3 8538 00007 9686

W9-BPS-947

LPB
FIC   FERRIS, MONICA
FER   Hanging By a Thread

DATE DUE

AUG 2 2 2012		
OCT 1 1 2012		
NOV 0 6 2013		
MAY 0 8 2014		
JUL 2 4 2015		
SEP 2 8 2015		

40820

Stockton Twp Public Library
140 W. Benton Ave.
Stockton, IL. 61085-1312
    (815) 947-2030

HANGING
BY A
THREAD

**Center Point
Large Print**

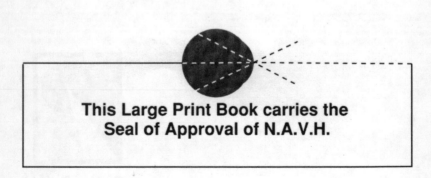

**This Large Print Book carries the
Seal of Approval of N.A.V.H.**

HANGING BY A THREAD

Monica Ferris

Center Point Publishing
Thorndike, Maine

This Center Point Large Print edition
is published in the year 2004 by arrangement with
The Berkley Publishing Group, a division of
Penguin Group (USA) Inc.

Copyright © 2003 by Mary Monica Kuhfeld.

All rights reserved.

The text of this Large Print edition is unabridged. In other
aspects, this book may vary from the original edition. Printed in
Thailand. Set in 16-point Times New Roman type.

ISBN 1-58547-450-9

Library of Congress Cataloging-in-Publication Data

Ferris, Monica.
    Hanging by a thread / Monica Ferris.--Center Point large print ed.
        p. cm.
    ISBN 1-58547-450-9 (lib. bdg. : alk. paper)
        1. Women detectives--Minnesota--Fiction. 2. Needlework--Fiction. 3. Minnesota--Fiction.
    4. Large type books. I. Title.

PS3566.U47H36 2004
813'.6--dc22

                                                                    2004000911

40820   8-4-07

40830 8-4-01

Acknowledgments

Some of the ghost stories told here are at least based on actual accounts made by real people. A Thursday knitting group is helping me improve my knitting skills or at least talk a better game. Mia McDavid read an early version of this novel and made some very helpful suggestions. And, of course, the Internet newsgroup rctn continues to be a valuable resource.

HANGING
BY A
THREAD

1

It was just after one on a dreary late-October day. Betsy had enjoyed September with its crisp, apple-scented air, and early October when the trees formed immense bouquets of bright autumn colors. She even liked it now, when her little town of Excelsior was seen through a waving crosshatch of bare tree limbs, as a strong wind ripped low-hanging clouds to tatters. It made her feel daring to go out in it, and grateful to come into a dry, heated place of her own.

Though Halloween was still a week away, last night it had snowed. The snow had turned to sleet and then rain. Autumn, stripped of its gaudy garments, was being hustled off the stage as Puritan winter entered stage north.

Today was Monday, and the Monday Bunch was in session around the library table in the middle of the floor of Betsy's needlework shop, Crewel World. An informal club of stitchers and gossips, there were five present this afternoon: Alice Skoglund, Martha Winters, young Emily Hame, newcomer Bershada Reynolds, and Comfort Leckie.

Chief clerk Godwin was presiding and shamelessly encouraging the gossip. He was a slender, handsome young man with bright blond hair cropped short and a carefully nurtured golden tan. "Arne Thorson should be *ashamed* of himself," he said. "That girl is young enough to be his *granddaughter!*"

11

Comfort, a widow in her late seventies who didn't look a day over sixty, said, "She seems happy enough." She peered closer at her work, a cross-stitch pattern of flowers. "Doggone, it takes me about three tries to get a really nice French knot." She began picking apart the one she'd just done.

Bershada offered, "On high-count linen like what you're using, I just put the needle through an adjoining space instead of back through the same hole." Bershada was a slim black woman, a freshly retired librarian who wore magnifying glasses halfway down her nose.

Betsy yearned to join them; she had a very fancy needlepoint Christmas stocking under way that she hoped to have finished in time to display in the shop. But there was a shipment of the new DMC colors to sort and put out, a phone call to be made to her supplier to find out why her order of padded-board easels hadn't come, and a reservation form to be filled out and check written for the Nashville Market next March.

She was nearly finished comparing the shipment of floss to the packing slip and her original order form when the front door went *Bing!* She looked up as it opened to admit a man in a yellow rain slicker. It was Foster Johns, her general contractor. He was tall and well built, in his late thirties, not handsome but with a pleasant face.

"Hello, Mr. Johns," she said with a smile, and then noticed with surprise the chilly silence that had fallen on the group around the table.

12

When the patch Joe Mickles had put on her building's roof just before signing the title over to her proved even less than temporary, she did what she should have done in the first place: hired an independent inspector. He told her she needed not a better patch but a whole new roof. She had tried and failed to get Joe to share in the expense. "It's your building now, kid," he'd said.

It was then she discovered there were roofs and roofs. What kind of insulation, and how much? Tar or membrane sealer? Local roofer or national chain? She didn't have time for all this!

So she got out her phone book and found a general contractor right here in Excelsior. She'd made an appointment and found a quiet man in an orderly office who had listened carefully to her description of her building and asked what sounded like intelligent questions. His last three clients spoke highly of his work. Relieved, she'd hired him to find the people it would take to get the work done.

And his early promise had been fulfilled; he'd been businesslike but not distant, knowledgeable without being overbearing, friendly but never familiar, always perfectly correct.

As the stink of tar finally faded from the neighborhood, he'd hired the same independent inspector to ensure the job was well finished before she wrote that final check. He said he'd bring him over sometime today.

Now she was surprised at the unfriendly silence that fell at his entry. The group at the table turned with almost military precision to follow his walk across the room. It was impossible he was unaware of the stony faces, but he ignored them. It was as if he were used to such a reception.

"The inspector is here to take a look at the roof, Ms. Devonshire," he said in his usual polite voice, stopping at the desk. "I'm sure he'll find everything in good order."

"I sure hope so," said Betsy. "How long will it take?"

"About an hour, unless he discovers a problem. I don't think he will; I've never had trouble with this roofer before. But I assume you want to wait for his report before making that final payment?"

"I think I should, don't you? Do you want to wait here while he does his thing?"

He turned briefly toward the people at the table. Alice Skoglund, her expression that of someone about to do something brave, nodded at him almost imperceptibly. He didn't return her tiny sign of recognition, but turned back to Betsy. "No, I've got some errands to run." He checked his watch. "I'll be back in ninety minutes, all right?"

"I hope to have that check waiting for you."

A look of pain crossed his face so swiftly, it was gone almost before she recognized it. "Me, too."

After he left, Betsy walked to the library table and asked, "Okay, what is it? I am about to give that man a large check. If you know of any reason why I shouldn't, please say so now."

Godwin said, "Oh, no, I'm *sure* he did a good job for

you!" He glanced at the women. "We all are! But honestly, Betsy, I wish you'd told me you were thinking of hiring him before you did."

"You know I ask you about anything to do with the shop. I didn't think that extended all the way to the roof," she said sharply. "Besides, you didn't leave the phone number of your hotel in Cancun."

Godwin blushed and said, "All the same, I wish you'd said something to me."

"Or to any of us," said Martha angrily. She was a short, plump woman in her mid-seventies, normally laughing and pleasant. Seeing her indignant like this was a warning Betsy didn't like.

Betsy frowned at her. "Why? If he isn't a crook, what's the problem?"

"Foster Johns is a murderer."

"I don't believe it!"

Godwin said, "It's true. I'd have warned you, Betsy, if I'd known you were thinking of hiring him. I thought you hired the roofer yourself."

"I told you I was having trouble deciding who to hire; that's why I went to a general contractor. Mr. Johns seemed very competent."

Martha said, "Competence has nothing to do with it. No one in town will have anything to do with Foster Johns since it happened five years ago."

"The accusation was never proven," said Alice in a low, firm voice. She was about Martha's age, a tall woman with big hands, broad shoulders, and a mannish jaw, currently set hard.

"Only because Mike Malloy is a stupid, incompetent

15

investigator," said Martha, still pink with indignation.

"Even so," said Betsy, "if it was never proved, why are you all so sure he's guilty?"

"Because he's the only one who could have done it," said Godwin.

Comfort added, "Certainly he was the only one with a motive." She had a very pleasant, quiet voice.

"Who did he murder, his wife?" asked Betsy.

Comfort finished another French knot using Bershada's suggestion and nodded with satisfaction. Without looking up, she said, "He murdered his mistress one night and a few nights later murdered her husband."

"He killed *two* people?"

Young Emily, nodding, said, "I can't believe no one warned you about him."

Betsy said, "Maybe because it's not a question that occurs to me when asking around about a contractor: 'By the way, has he ever murdered anyone?' I called him and he seemed to know his business, and his fee was reasonable. Not one of the references I called said don't hire him, he's a killer. And I like working with him, he seems very competent."

"No customers were from Excelsior, right?" said Godwin.

"Well, as a matter of fact, no," agreed Betsy.

"He has to go out of town for customers," said Martha. "No one from right around here will hire him, because we all know what he did."

Alice unset her heavy jaw to say, "Because it's everyone's *opinion* that he murdered those people.

16

There was never any proof."

Godwin said, "All right, it's true Malloy couldn't find the kind of evidence it would take to convict him before a jury of his peers. That's why he had to let him go. But it's not because it wasn't *there*, it's because he didn't look *hard* enough, or in the right *places*. I heard he nearly lost his job because he bungled the investigation."

"I've often said he should be busted back to patrol," offered Bershada, a trifle diffidently, as she was still feeling her way into this group.

Betsy nodded; she knew Investigator Malloy. "I'll grant that Mike's not the sharpest knife in the drawer," she said. "Still, it must have taken a depressingly large amount of incompetence to allow a man who has murdered twice to walk free." Free so that innocent shopowners could hire him to arrange repairs, restorations, and/or renovations of commercial properties. Betsy looked out the rain-spattered front window, but Foster Johns was already out of sight. It was almost an equally shattering thought that she, with a talent for uncovering amateur criminals, had found this alleged murderer to be an honest, trustworthy sort, with an attractive personality. Betsy tended to trust her feelings about people. How could she be so wrong?

2

What can you tell me about these people he murdered?" asked Betsy, sitting down at the table, her work forgotten.

Martha said, "They were Paul and Angela Schmitt. It was the old, old story. Angela was married to Paul but having an affair with Foster."

Alice said quietly, "I remember how shocked and sad Foster was the day Angela was found dead. I know everyone thinks he did it"—she looked at Martha—"but there is someone sitting right here at this table who knows the value of 'everyone thinks.'"

Martha, who had once been popularly suspected of a double homicide, said in a shocked voice, "That's different!"

"No, it isn't." Alice looked at Betsy. "You told me that one reason you look into crime is not so much to discover the guilty as to rescue the innocent. If Foster Johns is innocent, he certainly could use rescuing. His life has been extremely difficult since those murders."

Godwin said, "Don't even think about it, Betsy."

"Never fear, it's about to become the busiest time of year for me. I don't have time for distractions." Reminded, she stood and went back to the desk.

"All he had to do was move away—" began Emily.

Alice said, "Do you think if he had gone away, he wouldn't have lived in fear the rest of his life that someone from his old hometown would show up and

18

tell that story to his new friends? Anyway, he has a business here that took him years to build! If he tried to sell it, who'd give him a good price? No one!"

"Well, if he's guilty," said Bershada, "that would be about what he deserves!"

"That's *right,*" declared Godwin. "Are you saying he should be treated nicely, Alice? He should be *in jail!* And since that hasn't happened, the least we can do is cut him right out of our lives! It was *horrible* that a man Angela Schmitt loved and trusted *murdered* her!" He turned to Betsy. "She was the *sweetest* little thing," he said, "like a timid child, and Paul loved her for it— he was very protective of her."

Emily said, "I remember him. He had that kind of face that's always smiling. He'd see you coming and he'd always say hello. He loved Angela and bought her anything she wanted."

" 'A man may smile and smile and be a villain,' Shakespeare wrote," said Alice.

"So what?" said Godwin. "It wasn't true in this case. He even took that second job in the gift shop so he could be near her."

"She couldn't have been afraid of him," said Martha, "if she started an affair with another man."

Betsy put down the packing list to ask, "Why did she start an affair with Foster if Paul was such a wonderful husband?"

Godwin said, "The lure of the new and exciting, I suppose." He made a sad-comical face. "Of course, I'm no expert in heterosexual affairs of the heart, but are they all that different from my own?" Godwin was gay, and his flirtatious ways sometimes infuriated his partner. "But she found out the hardest way that the grass isn't always greener on the wrong side of the fence."

"Possibly Foster didn't want her to leave her husband," suggested Bershada. "This way, Paul bought the cake and Foster got the icing."

"Well, that brings up another question," said Betsy. "Suppose she was going to leave him. That's a common pattern: The husband finds out that his wife wants a divorce, so he murders her and then himself. Couldn't that have happened here?"

"No," said Emily. "Paul's death was a murder, all right. There was some kind of fight in his house the night he was shot."

Martha said, "And the gun was never found."

Emily said, "*I* think Angela came to her senses and told Foster she wanted to break it off. There was a quarrel, and he murdered her. And he was so mad at Paul, he murdered him, too."

Comfort said thoughtfully, "There are women who, for whatever reason, pick domineering men. She married one, and when he made her unhappy, she chose another one as a lover."

Betsy said, "But Foster doesn't strike me as domineering. Maybe it's more that she was the kind of woman who liked to make her man jealous. Maybe she was making Paul angry by taking up with Foster."

Alice said, "I never, ever saw her do anything that would make me think she was a flirt or a tease. She was quiet and a little standoffish."

"How sure are you that she really was having an affair?" asked Betsy. "If it was all a tease—"

Godwin said, "Oh, Foster admitted it! It was on the news and everything. He probably seduced the poor thing."

Betsy said, "While my relationship with Foster is strictly business—"

"Yes, how *is* Morrie?" asked Godwin sweetly. He'd been delighted and amused to learn Betsy had a beau. Morrie Stephens was a police investigator with the Minnetonka Police Department. He had met Betsy last summer and admired her sleuthing ways. They were seeing a lot of each other and he was already hinting he wanted her to sell Crewel World and move to Fort Myers with him, after he retired this winter. Betsy hadn't told Godwin this not-so-amusing detail.

"Hush," she said, blushing lightly. "I'm about to make a point here. Am I so wrong about Foster, is he the sort who goes about seducing shy married women for sport?"

"Well, no, he didn't impress me that way," said Alice. "I was surprised to find out about him and Angela. But when I was married to a pastor, I found out things that happen between men and women you wouldn't believe."

"The thing is, there isn't any other explanation," said Comfort. "No one else was close to Angela, no one else had any reason at all to murder her."

"Except Paul, if he had found out his wife was making a fool of him with Foster Johns," said Betsy. "Any husband—or wife, for that matter—is apt to be very angry when they learn something like that." Betsy had divorced her husband when she found that he had been repeatedly unfaithful. "So it's logical to suppose that if Paul found out about Foster, he murdered Angela. Then perhaps Foster, in a rage, murdered Paul. That would make sense."

Martha said, "But the police said the same gun was used to kill both of them."

They looked at Betsy to explain that, if she could. So of course she tried. "Well, okay, still say Paul murdered his wife. Foster, in a rage, went to see Paul, who naturally became frightened and pulled out his gun. They fought over it, and Foster got it and shot Paul."

That made sense, and the challenging looks faded.

"But then why didn't Foster call the police?" asked Emily. "Isn't that self-defense?"

Betsy, remembering the cool, competent way Foster had handled the complex details of getting the building permits, hiring a roofer and the company to haul away the remains of the old roof, and while he was about it someone to replace the gutters, frowned. The Foster she thought she had come to know would certainly call the police if he had shot someone in self-defense. She thought a bit, then asked, "Why suspect only Foster Johns in this case? Couldn't someone else have murdered Paul Schmitt? Doesn't Angela have family in the area who might have avenged her murder?"

"Her father lives in Florida most of the year. He was down there when she was murdered, and was just about to fly back when Paul was killed," said Godwin. "She has two brothers, but one lives in California, and the other was overseas with the Army. So, you see, there really isn't anyone else. Paul wasn't the kind to blow his cool. He wasn't as sweet as Emily thinks, but who is?"

Emily blushed but said, "He was too!"

"He managed that Scandinavian gift shop really well," Godwin continued, "expanded their reach into British and Irish stock, which improved their bottom line—he was bragging about it at a party. I can't think of a single enemy he had. And, of course, no one in his right mind had any reason to hate Angela."

"Maybe a robbery?" suggested Betsy.

Martha said, "Well, I think that's what the police thought, right at first. Angela was alone when she was shot there, she was closing up that night. But she wouldn't have resisted if someone came in with a gun, she wasn't the least brave. Anyway, nothing was taken."

Alice said, "That's because the gun being fired brought people's attention, so whoever it was had to leave or be caught."

Martha said, "That's right, a bullet broke a window, and the bookstore's right on Water Street, so there were a lot of people who came rushing to see what was going on. And of course everyone thought it was a robbery. But then Paul was shot, and at home. So then everyone thought what you suggested, Betsy, that Paul shot her and then himself. But when we heard about the fight, and that the police couldn't find the gun, we knew it was something else."

Godwin said, "And that time it wasn't Malloy doing

the investigating. Paul lived in Navarre, that's where he was shot."

Martha said, "But Mike was over there because they thought there might be a link between Paul's and Angela's murders. And there was: The same gun was used in both murders."

Comfort said, "I remember hearing on the news the morning after it happened that a neighbor heard shooting at the Schmitt house and called the police."

"You meant there was a gunfight?" asked Betsy.

"No, no, there was just one gun involved, but there were several shots fired."

"That's right, I remember reading that in the Minneapolis newspaper," said Godwin. "The neighbors were too scared to look out their windows, or there might have been a description of Foster running away or a license plate number or something. But there wasn't. And that's one reason he wasn't arrested. Which is too bad; Paul Schmitt was shot two or three times, so it wasn't an easy death."

"Dreadful," murmured Emily, and there was a little silence.

Betsy said, "Wait, it doesn't make sense that Foster would murder Angela and then Paul. In fact . . ." Her frown deepened. "I suppose I can see Foster going to Paul to tell him he was in love with Angela and demanding Paul divorce her, then getting in a fight and killing Paul. And I suppose it could happen that his mistress was so upset about it, she threatened to turn him in, so he killed her, too. But that's not the order this happened in. I suppose it's possible a man might be so exasperated and infuriated with his mistress that he murders her. But then, having done that, why round it off by murdering her husband? I mean, he's so handy as a suspect, isn't he?"

"But maybe Paul knew Foster did it, maybe he even had some kind of proof, so Foster had to kill him," suggested Bershada.

"There you go," said Godwin, his eyes lighting up at this evidence of clever thinking. He smiled at Bershada.

"Instead of going to the police?" asked Betsy.

"Well, maybe he wanted to protect his wife's reputation," said Comfort.

"Oh, that's so old-fashioned!" scoffed Godwin. "People nowadays don't care a rat's right ear for things like that."

"Only Foster knows why it happened in that order," said Martha darkly. "And he's not telling."

Alice squared her shoulders and asked Betsy, "Could it be that Foster didn't commit any murder at all?"

"Why are you so eager to defend him, anyhow?" demanded Godwin.

"Because . . . because I was paying attention before all this happened," said Alice. "I think Paul might not have been a good husband. And I saw the way Foster behaved after Angela was murdered. He didn't act the least bit guilty."

"That's because he has nerves of steel and a heart of ice," said Comfort.

"I mean he was sad and upset, not calm and cool," said Alice.

Bershada said, "Well, if I murdered someone, I'd be sad and upset, too. Anyway, if he didn't do it, who did?"

Alice said, "I don't know. You all think you know Foster did it, but the police couldn't find enough evidence to charge him, much less convict him. That has to mean something, doesn't it?"

"Not with Mike involved in the investigations," said Martha pointedly.

"Well, we're not the clever ones when it comes to solving mysteries, Betsy is. Think for a minute, Betsy. Who do you think did it?"

"Thinking wouldn't help," said Betsy frankly. "There's not enough information for me—"

She was interrupted by the annoying *Bing!* of the front door. Foster Johns, his back to them while he closed the door, turned and saw the faces turned toward him. But his voice was calm when he said, "The inspector finished quicker than he thought he would and came looking for me. He seems to think everything is fine. What are you going to do about it?"

3

I 'll write you a check after I talk to the inspector," said Betsy.

The relief in Johns's eyes was palpable. "He's outside," Johns said, and turned and opened the door. Its *Bing!* sounded loud in the rigid silence of the shop, and Betsy noted irrelevantly that she'd forgotten to turn on the radio when she opened up that morning. She glanced around at the table and Alice caught her eye with a tiny, encouraging nod.

At Johns's gesture, a short man in heavy blue coveralls came in. "Ms. Devonshire," he said with a little nod, removing his red hunter's hat to reveal a bald head surrounded by white hair.

"Mr. Jurgens." Betsy nodded back.

He frowned at the silent group at the table. "Is there a problem?"

"I don't think so," said Betsy. "Unless you found something else wrong with my roof." Betsy had thought the job done two weeks ago, but the inspector had discovered a pair of flaws, necessitating a removal of part of the new tarred covering, replacement of some of the insulation, and then fresh hot tar being applied to the patches. This, Foster Johns assured Betsy, was not really unusual, and the patch would be as sound as if it were original to the roof.

"The repair is fine. They did a good job—that roof should do well for prob'ly twenty years, if not more." He unbuttoned the top of his coveralls, revealing a red plaid shirt, and fumbled in a pocket for a thin sheaf of papers folded lengthwise. "Here's my report."

Betsy took the papers and glanced them over. Computer printouts, they included a copy of his first report saying she needed a new roof, then the one describing the flaws he'd found, and on top the newest report indicating the roof was now properly done and resealed. He had signed this one in thick, soft pencil and dated it today.

"These look fine," said Betsy. "Thank you." The inspector put his hat back on, glanced again at the people around the table, and departed.

"If you can wait here a minute, Mr. Johns," said Betsy, "I'll go upstairs and get my checkbook."

"May I come with you? I'd like a word with you, in private."

"Sure—no, wait a minute." Betsy glanced at her watch. It was nearly two, and she hadn't had lunch yet. "How about I go get my checkbook and then we both go to Antiquity Rose for a bowl of soup? Or have you had lunch?"

He hesitated, then nodded. "Not yet."

Antiquity Rose was a house converted to a tea and antique shop. It had an excellent kitchen, which was currently featuring a hearty potato-cheese soup. Betsy had hers with a bran muffin. Foster chose the fat, warm breadstick.

After a few spoonfuls, Betsy said, "Did you bring your bill with you?"

"Yes, but that's not the problem I wanted to talk to you about."

"No? What's the problem?"

Foster looked across the little table, his face a mix of desperation and hope. "I heard you do private investigations for people falsely charged with crimes."

"That's approximately true. Who's in trouble?"

His smile was wry. "Don't tell me they didn't give you an earful while I was gone. Because of people like them, I've been living in hell for five years and eleven days."

"Ah," said Betsy. "Yes, they told me about Paul and Angela Schmitt."

"I was hoping that if I could get just one person in town to give me a chance, then they'd start to come around. But I guess now you're sorry I took advantage of your ignorance."

Betsy's lips tightened. "That's not true."

"Of course, if I murdered two people, nothing could be bad enough to be worse than I deserve. But I didn't. I've done everything I can think of to show people I'm an honest citizen, but nothing's worked. Then someone told me about you—"

"Who?" interrupted Betsy. "Who told you?"

"Jurgens, the inspector. He told me you solved your sister's murder and another murder up on the North Shore. 'She's real slick,' is how Jurgens put it. I hope he's right and this is something you're willing to do for me." Indeed, he looked so hopeful, Betsy's heart was again wrenched, and all her promises about this being too busy a time of year for sleuthing began to crumble. Still, she held herself to a mere nod, and he continued, "I don't know what you charge, but if you can clear my name, any amount is worth it. How much do you want as a retainer?"

"Nothing. I don't have a private investigator's license, and I wouldn't dream of taking money from you."

He tossed his spoon into his bowl and sat back. "I'm sorry you feel like that."

"Wait a minute, I didn't say I wouldn't try to help. I am willing to look into your problem, but it will be

29

strictly as an amateur." Hope flared on his face—here was no heart of ice or nerve of steel—and she added, "I just hope you aren't in a big rush. It will probably be after the first of the year before I can give your case the attention it deserves. All I can do now is try to gather some basic information."

He nodded. "I've waited this long, I can be patient a while longer. What do you want to know?"

She asked, "First, have you thought about hiring a real private investigator?"

"I did that. He charged me three thousand dollars and all he could tell me was that Paul Schmitt probably abused Angela. I already knew that to be a fact."

Betsy said, "It's been five years. If I start asking questions, people are going to recall some sordid details. Are you sure you want me bringing the whole mess up again?"

"What again? It's never gone away. I'll tell you anything I can. What do you need from me to begin with?"

Betsy thought. "Let's start with Angela. Tell me about her."

Foster leaned forward and a slow smile formed as he cast his mind back. "I didn't mean to fall in love with her," he said. "I don't even know exactly when it happened. I do know that it started when I said something to her on the steps after church one Sunday about it finally getting warm enough to do some work outdoors, and she thought I meant gardening. I said, 'No, I own a construction company,' which I did back then, and we were making a joke about the misunderstanding when her husband came from out of nowhere and yanked her away so hard, she dropped her purse. The look on his face surprised me, it was so full of anger. But I thought I was mistaken. I mean, I thought I knew Paul, we'd ushered together a few times, and I'd had a few conversations with him about roofing— he was a good amateur carpenter. He was one of those guys who almost always has a grin on his face, like he's got the point of a joke the rest of us don't. So that look that day was surprising. I actually remember trying to decide if it was the angle of the sun putting a funny shadow on his face. You see, he was always willing to lend a hand, jump-start a car, bring groceries to a shut-in, like that.

"But while I was surprised by him, I was surprised even more by the look on her face as she went off with him, like she was scared to death of what would happen when he got her home. Even weirder, when he noticed it, he shook her arm and she all of a sudden looked fine." He shrugged.

"At the time, of course, I didn't think of it that way, that he was ordering her to wipe that look off her face. It was only later I learned what a son of a bitch he was, excuse my French. That she was right to be scared.

"We were born the same year, Angela and me, and Paul was two years older. I went to high school with them both, though I never dated her—I was into big, cushy blonds back then, so I didn't see her as my type. She was just a bit of a thing, and dark-haired. But she was pretty enough, and I think could have been popular if she put herself out some more. But she was shy, hardly said anything to anyone in school. I went on to get my degree in architectural engineering, but she dropped out of college to marry Paul.

"Anyhow, the Sunday after I talked to Angela about the weather, Alice Skoglund said it was sad how Angela seemed so unhappy nowadays, and something about the way she said it made me think of that scared look. So I kind of kept my eye on her for the next few weeks, and once I paid attention, I could see Angela wasn't just unhappy, she was scared. So I took to talking to her when Paul wasn't around, which was like a minute here and a minute there—he was generally right with her. But I kept trying to find out what was going on. Pretty soon she trusted me enough to really talk to me. And soon after I got the hint from her that he was abusing her. I got mad on her behalf, and told her to walk out, just leave him, go down to Florida to stay with her parents; but she said she was afraid of what he might do.

"By then I wasn't just out to rescue a fellow Lutheran; it was getting personal. So I paid attention, I got to know her schedule, and we'd meet while she was grocery shopping or on her way to and from work, friends' houses, like that. He was always checking up on her, phoning her, making her account for her time, so it was tricky." He smiled. "But I'm an efficient scheduler, and we got pretty good at it. Then I started pressuring her to leave him for me. I said I'd send her to live with my parents in North Carolina, or my sister in Las Vegas, until he gave up looking for her, but she said he'd never give up, and when he found her, he'd kill her *and* whoever was giving her shelter, so she just couldn't do that. I was even looking into those ways of giving someone a new identity when it happened." His face tightened.

"You're saying he's the one who killed her," said Betsy.

"Of course. There was no one else, how could there be? He never let her get close enough to anyone, so there was no one else to love her or hate her enough to do that."

"You managed."

"And he found out."

"How do you know?"

"Because she phoned me from work the day it happened, to warn me to keep away from her, that Paul had gone from suspecting she was fooling around to being sure she was, and that I was involved. He'd actually started writing down the mileage on her car, and it didn't match the driving she was supposed to be doing, so he figured she was going somewhere she shouldn't. Which she was, of course. He'd seen me going into the bookstore and talking to her, and she smiled at me in a way that, he said, told him all he needed to know. That night it was her turn to stay and close up the shop, and normally we would have a few minutes together. But this time I walked up Water Street a little after five, just to look in the window and see her. It was pouring rain and when I waved at her, I got water up my sleeve—funny the things you remember. She waved back and I went on up the street. I wish I'd gone in, I wish . . ." He twisted his head, dismissing that futile thought. "He worked just

33

two doors down from her, did you know that?"

Betsy said, "Yes, in the Heritage gift shop on the corner." Betsy could see it in her mind's eye, it was light red brick and went around the corner in a curve just broad enough to accommodate a door. Its big windows were generally full of imported dishes, sweaters or dresses, and glassware.

"He took that job to spy on her. He did freelance computer programming in an office in their house for very respectable pay; and he did some freelance home repairs, carpentry mostly, for which he got paid under the table. Not paying taxes made up for not getting union wages. He didn't need that job at the gift shop."

"How long did Angela work at the bookstore?"

"Not quite two years. She'd begged and pleaded with him and he finally said she could get a part-time job. It wasn't for the money, not entirely, she just wanted out of the house. But he couldn't stand the thought of her meeting strange men all day long, so right after she started, he got that job so he could watch her." Foster smiled. "He wanted to work in the pet shop right next door, but she was allergic to cat hair, and he'd've come home with it on him. And he couldn't work in the place on the other side of the bookstore, it's a beauty parlor." He ripped his bread stick into three pieces. "There's the proof he was some kind of nut, taking that job just to spy on her. She was never, ever unfaithful to him."

Betsy's eyebrows went up at that, and he said, "I mean it. We wanted to—God, how we wanted to! But he made her carry a cell phone and he called her about every fifteen minutes when she wasn't home or in the bookstore, where was she, what was she doing, who was there with her. He said he loved her, but it was a crazy love. He was crazy, insane."

He looked up at Betsy. "So you see, when she was shot, I knew it was him. It had to be. It wasn't me, and there wasn't anyone else. The police thought so, too, when they figured out it wasn't a robbery. But he'd rigged some kind of alibi, so when Gloria in the bookstore told them about me coming in to buy more books in six months than I'd bought in five years, and talking like a friend to someone I ignored when her husband was around . . ." He made a pained face. "Funny how there's always a slip somewhere, isn't it? Gloria knew me because her husband hired me to remodel their house back when I was just starting out, and she's a member of my church, which is where she saw me not speaking to Angela in front of Paul. We tried so hard to be cool in front of Paul that she noticed.

"Anyhow, Mike Malloy came to talk to me. I told him that I was very fond of Angela, that she'd told me her husband was crazy jealous and beat her up every time the mood took him. I told him Paul had just found out about me and Angela, so it had to be Paul who shot her."

Betsy said, "But then Paul was shot."

Johns nudged a fragment of breadstick with a forefinger. "Turned everything on its head. Now they were looking for someone with a motive to shoot both of them. And the closest they can come is me."

"So why didn't they arrest you?"

"They did. But they had to let me go, because while I was near the bookstore that night, I had an alibi for the night Paul was shot."

"An *alibi?*"

"Paul and my cleaning lady provided it between them. Damnedest thing. He phoned me at my office and said he wanted to see me. Well, I didn't want to see him, but he said he had evidence of who murdered Angela. He said the cops would think he cooked it up, but if I was the one who brought it to the cops, they'd believe me. He said, 'It'll help you, too, Foster, because the cops are sure that if it isn't me, then it's probably you.' I asked him, 'Who did it?'—not believing him, of course—and he said, 'It's someone who's after me. He killed Angela because he knows how much I loved her and he wants me to suffer before he kills me.' And I asked him again, 'Who is it?' and he said I wouldn't believe it, he had to show me, and that's why he wanted to talk to me in person about it.

"Well, I didn't know whether he had anything or not, but I didn't want him in my house, so I said, 'Come to my office with your proof.' And we set a time of nine o'clock that night. Yes, it occurred to me that he might do something really stupid, like shoot me, too. But what if he really had something? I owned a little tape recorder, it had a switch position for sound activation; it stops when it's quiet, then starts when people start talking. I put it in a desk drawer I left a little bit open, figuring that if he admits he did it, or if he pulls something, there will be a recording.

"You know my place, it started life as a little gas station up on Third and Water back in the thirties." Betsy nodded—the design of the little stucco building with its steep tile roof announced its origins. "I've got a reception area in front, and in back a room for the guy who helps me do estimates and supervises the crews at work and my own office, which I also use for meetings. I went out for supper at Hilltop about six-thirty, and since I had nothing else to do, I went back to my office. We have a cleaning lady but she was already done when I got back, and that saved my hide."

"How was that?" asked Betsy

"Well, we'd been asked to take a look at the old Ace Hardware store—this was before the fire, and the owner wanted to upgrade the apartments over the store. He wanted my ideas and an estimate on remodeling. I hadn't had a chance to look at the specs yet, so I got out the notes I'd taken when we talked, and the plans and my calculator, and did some work while I waited for Paul Schmitt to come by. Which he didn't. At nine twenty I phoned his house, and when there was no answer, I assumed he was on his way over. But he wasn't. I finally went home a little after ten, and the police came and woke me up around eleven. They wanted to know where I was between nine and nine forty-five and I said I was in my office. Alone, of course."

Betsy asked, "So how did your cleaning lady help give you an alibi?"

"She told the cops that when she left my building at seven forty-five, my desk was clear and my office was perfectly clean, but when I took the cops back over there, the wastebasket was half full of wadded-up notes, and the top of my desk and a table were covered with plans and blueprints and estimates, and there were a couple of drawings pinned up on my bulletin board that weren't there before. I'm a messy worker, and when I'm working on a job, I tend to leave things out, for which I thank God—and for not staying until I finished, because I would've put things away. I mean, it's not the greatest alibi in the world, but it was good enough. That and the fact that there wasn't a mark on me or any blood on my clothes, because there had been a knockdown drag-out at Paul's house."

"Did the police find the evidence Paul said he had about who murdered Angela?"

"The detective never mentioned that they found anything. Not that he would have, but I don't know that anyone else was ever questioned about it. And they never arrested anyone else, damn it to hell."

"Do you think Paul ever had any evidence of who really murdered Angela?"

"I don't know. My first thought was that Paul set it up somehow, trashed his living room and ran into things until he was all beat up, then shot himself."

"Now wait a minute," objected Betsy, "surely the police could tell the difference between someone running into something and the marks of a fist!"

"Maybe he punched himself in the face." Seeing her doubtful expression, he said earnestly, "Angela convinced me Paul was crazy," said Foster. "Seriously crazy, as in mentally ill. He liked to get mad at her, she said, so he'd have an excuse to beat her. He'd set her up so no matter what she said he could convince himself he had a right to be angry. He'd come home in some kind of weird mood and she'd know that before bedtime, he'd find a reason to hit her. He never let anyone else see how things would get to him, so when he was angry about something, he'd still be nice and smiling to other people, but he'd come home and take it out on Angela. And he didn't feel pain like normal people. She said one time he cut his knuckle on her tooth and wouldn't even put a Band-Aid on it until she complained he was getting blood all over the sheets."

"All right, buying for a minute your theory that Paul was capable of beating himself up, where did the gun that shot him go?"

"Yes, that's what throws it all in the toilet, doesn't it? The damn gun is gone. So maybe Paul was right, he had an enemy who really hated him, who murdered Angela to torture him and then beat him up before shooting him."

"Have you any idea who that might be?" asked Betsy.

"Not an inkling. But"—he leaned forward to point a knobby index finger at Betsy—"don't let the people you talk to make a saint of him, talking about his good deeds and that smile he always had on his face. Angela told me that his smile was like the smile of a dolphin. His face was just made that way, a kind of birth defect, it didn't mean a thing. He had to make an effort to not smile. He would smile in his sleep and he would smile while he was punching her."

4

Betsy gently rubbed the surface of a Christmas tree ornament done in shades of antique gold and deep red. Very Velvet was a narrow, ribbonlike fiber with a short, dense nap, luxurious to the touch. Her stocking design was painted on canvas by an artist named Marcy, and depicted a branch of long-needled pine hung with very elaborate ornaments and tinsel. She should be doing her books, but she was in a race with the calendar to get this stocking done in time to be "finished," cut from its surrounding of blank canvas, lined, and sewn to a backing that would turn it into a real Christmas stocking.

Not that she would ever put anything in the stocking, of course. Such a beautiful and labor-intensive object would be strictly for display. She had other painted canvases by Marcy, and would hang this in her shop among them to show customers how lovely the finished project could be.

Jill said, "Don't rub the fuzz off," but not with any rancor. Jill was a police officer, a young woman whose Scandinavian heritage showed both in her ash-blond coloring and the low emotional content of her speech. She loved subtle jokes, cross-country skiing, and needlepoint, and was pleased to see Betsy doing something elaborate in the last area.

Betsy held the stocking at arm's length by its scroll bars so she could admire it. The colors and pattern of this piece were already so complex that she'd decided to do all of it in basic basketweave, and add interest by using different fibers: overdyed silks, perle cotton, metallics, wool, a difficult tubular ribbon called Crystal Rays, and Very Velvet. Each fiber caught the light differently, adding depth and interest to the work.

Jill, working on her own needlepoint canvas of a Siamese cat looking at itself in a mirror, asked, "Are you going to try to help Foster Johns?"

Betsy replied, "I'm going to look into it a bit." She cut a length of black wool and threaded her needle—there being no other color she hadn't used, she was doing the background of the stocking in black. "I don't have time to do a really intensive investigation, it's about to become very busy in the shop—I hope."

"So you don't think he did it?"

"I don't know what to think. What do you know about the night it happened?"

"Which murder?"

"Angela's."

"I wasn't on duty, so I wasn't one of the first responders, but I got called in to stand guard at the back door of the bookshop."

Excelsior was a small town, with a small police department. All sworn officers had to be prepared to respond to a call to duty at any time. Fortunately, in law-abiding Excelsior, this was a rare occurrence. Jill tilted her canvas back and forth under the light to see if the next few stitches were in the same shade of cream she was using or a lighter one. "I was new to the force at the time," she continued, "so I didn't dare say

41

what I thought—that Malloy should call in the BCA. Those state fellows run a lot of crime scenes, while murder is a rare event around here."

"Did you get to see the crime scene?" Betsy ran her needle through some completed stitches on the back to anchor the yarn, then poked her needle through.

"No, but I got an earful, then and later. No sign of a struggle. Apparently two shots were fired, but Angela was shot just once, from behind, and the bullet went through her chest and out the front window of the bookstore."

Betsy frowned. Someone had mentioned a broken window, but not this horrible detail. "Out the window—is that possible?"

"Sure, with a magnum-style bullet. It punched a big hole in Angela, and a bigger hole in the glass."

"Oh, gah!" said Betsy, never fond of gory details. "You said two shots were fired. Could someone have shot Angela and then fired out the window?"

"Why would someone do that?"

"I don't know. Maybe he shot out the window and then shot Angela?"

"Again, why?"

"I don't know. But why two shots?"

"Oh, I thought you meant on purpose. I think he shot at Angela twice, missed the first time and got her the second. But they never found either slug," Jill said.

"That's odd."

"Yes, it is. Of course, Mike didn't find the second shell casing, either. His report says one shot, it went through Angela and out the window. One of the store employees found the second shell casing months later, when they were replacing some bookshelves."

"So you don't think the murderer shot out the window on purpose?" Betsy asked.

"Why would he do that? It called attention to the bookstore. The 911 operators reported three calls in less than two minutes. One said it was a bomb, one said it was a drive-by, one said it was a robbery in progress. Like most first calls, they were all mistaken. It wasn't a bomb, the bullet came from inside the store, and nothing was stolen. Mike suspected for a while that it was an attempted robbery, and when the window blew out, the would-be robber ran out the back before alarmed passersby could catch him."

"Does he still think that's a valid theory?" Betsy put a single angled stitch beside the teardrop-shaped ornament.

"Not really. Not since Paul was killed so soon after. But he still thinks Angela must have let the person in, because both doors were locked when the police arrived."

"So how did the murderer get out?"

"The back door didn't have the deadbolt keyed shut, just the Yale, which you can open by hand from inside and which locks itself when you close the door."

"Fingerprints?"

"The only ones found were hers and the owner's. Gloves, probably."

"Did she ordinarily let people into the store after it closed?"

43

"I wouldn't think so. You don't let people in after you close, do you? Unless it's an emergency."

"True. And more people think it's an emergency that they need another skein of DMC 758 than that they need a copy of *The Ten Stupid Things Women Do to Mess Up Their Lives*," said Betsy.

"Malloy might agree, except for the part about needing an emergency skein of DMC floss. But you can see why, when Malloy and his partner went to tell Paul about his wife, they had some hope of arresting him for her murder."

"You mean Paul wasn't standing outside the bookstore demanding to know what was going on?"

"No, they found him doing paperwork in the gift shop."

"Hmmm."

"Why hmmm?" asked Jill.

"Because he is alleged to have taken that job just so he could keep an eye on Angela. Presumably a fuss of any sort would have him right out there taking a look. There were sirens, right?"

"Oh, yes, lots of sirens."

"So why didn't he come running to see what was going on?"

"I don't know. Maybe he was hard of hearing. Oh, wait a minute. It was pouring rain that evening, with lots of thunder and lightning. It's possible the racket covered up what was going on. I remember that night, it had snowed once, so seemed weird to be having a thunderstorm instead of a blizzard. I remember that because I was worried about standing outside in the storm—but also because that storm gave Paul his alibi."

"It did? How?"

"Well, if he'd gone from the gift shop to the bookstore and back, he'd've gotten soaked, even though it's only two doors down. But he was bone dry, hair, clothes, and shoes. He'd brought a raincoat with him to work, because the forecast was for thunderstorms, but it was dry, too. He was looking good for that murder, so they really searched for wet clothes he might have changed out of, for a hair dryer, plastic garbage bags with head and arm holes, any evidence he'd been out in that rain, and didn't find a thing. And no one saw him outside the gift shop. Despite the rain, there were people on the street, and some of them knew Paul by sight."

"So if it wasn't Paul, and it wasn't a robber . . ." said Betsy.

"Yes. And Foster was seen on Water Street right about the time it happened."

They stitched in silence for a while, then Betsy said, "Did you get called to the scene again when Paul was murdered?"

"No. He and Angela lived in Navarre. The police force out there called in Malloy, of course, when they identified Paul, because of Angela; so some of what happened got back to us. I heard there was clear evidence of a fight, a broken mirror, overturned furniture, blood spatters. Paul was shot twice, once in the leg and again in the head. The same gun was used in both murders, and it was never found." Jill put her stitching down to frown in thought for a few moments.

"What?" asked Betsy.

"What I think is, it's a shame that no one saw Foster in Navarre the night Paul was killed, the way people here saw him on Water Street."

"Maybe they didn't see him because he wasn't there. Foster told me he was in his office, waiting for a meeting with Paul that never happened."

Jill said, "I don't think I ever heard that."

"Foster says Paul called him and said he had evidence that would clear both of them of Angela's murder. Paul said he had proof of who really murdered his wife."

"Who did he say it was?"

"He told Foster he had to see the proof to believe it, that it was someone no one thought it could be."

Jill asked, "And you believe that story?"

"I don't know what to believe. Foster said Angela told him that Paul was a very strange person. It's a weird alibi Foster has, too. But Foster says the police found evidence he was in his office after the cleaning lady left. On the other hand, it's hard to imagine that Foster would agree to meet the man he cuckolded, a man he described as a crazy wife-beater."

"Did he tell anyone he was meeting Paul?"

"That's a good question, I'll ask him that next time I see him. Jill, did you ever hear or see anything that would make you think Paul was insane?"

"That's a funny question."

"I know. But Foster said Angela was afraid of what he might do if she left him, that Paul was dangerous.

He said Paul was always grinning, even when he was sad or angry."

Jill stopped stitching to close her eyes and think. "I remember that smile," she said at last. "But I didn't think it was crazy, I just thought he was a happy person. It wasn't one of those grins that don't reach the eyes, like you see sometimes. Paul's eyes squinched up, too." She considered a bit more. "He seemed like a happy, friendly person to me."

"That's two very different pictures. How well did you know him?"

"Not all that well."

"Who was Paul's best friend?"

"I don't know."

"Who does know?"

Jill smiled faintly. "Well, I'm sure the Bureau of Criminal Apprehension looked into his past pretty thoroughly, but I don't know how you could access their records."

"Do you have a connection in the BCA who might look for me?"

"Nope. Now you see, if you were a real police investigator, you could just call the BCA and ask to take a look at their files on the case."

"If I were really a police investigator, then Crewel World would be owned by someone who wouldn't let you return unused needlepoint wool."

Jill said with every appearance of deadpan sincerity, "There's a downside to everything, I guess."

The next day, Betsy phoned Alice Skoglund. "Hello,

Betsy," she said in her deep voice. "What may I do for you?"

"I want to ask you a question about Paul Schmitt."

A bit warily she asked, "What about Mr. Schmitt?"

"He was a long-time member of your church, wasn't he?"

"Well . . . yes, why?"

"I was wondering if you knew someone who was a good friend of his."

Alice didn't reply at once. Then she said, "I don't think I know of any."

"Think hard, Alice. This is important."

Alice had the curious trait of falling into what seemed like a noisy, deep-breathing coma when thinking, and suddenly the sounds of that were carried through the receiver at Betsy's ear. After a minute it stopped, and Alice said, "Well, he used to go hunting with Vern Miller and his sons, Jory and Alex. Paul and Jory are about the same age, and they were in the same Sunday-school class for several years. Paul and Alex were friends until Paul married Angela, but as far as I know, Vern and Jory stayed friends with Paul right up until Paul's death. Jory works for his father in that garage he runs over on Third. They'll probably be able to tell you who was Paul's best friend—if he had one."

Betsy had been to that garage, a scabrous place converted from a livery stable. It didn't sell gasoline, just did repairs on older vehicles, the kind without computer chips or built-in VCRs. Though she had heard he was very talented, Betsy would not allow Vern, who was built on the approximate lines of a shell for a large naval gun, and was about as intelligent, to touch her old Mercury Tracer. And of course her new Buick was outside his expertise.

So he watched her walk into his little office with a frown of puzzlement.

"Help you?" he offered in his deep, gruff voice. He was an old man, his face deeply creased, his white hair both overgrown and thinning. But his sloping shoulders were heavy, and his filthy overalls and black fingernails indicated he was still a working man.

"Is Jory here?" she asked. "I'd like to talk to both of you for a few minutes, if you can spare them, about Paul Schmitt."

Without rising he threw his head back and roared, *"Jory!"* His office was built into a corner of the workshop with old boards and chicken wire, he could have called his son with far less effort than that.

"What?!?" came the reply, equally loud, equally needlessly.

"C'mere!" He sat back in his ancient, battered chair behind a dirty, cluttered desk and smiled at her. "He'll be right in."

A minute later a man in his mid-thirties came in. He was slimmer than Vern, but not by much, and not much taller. Though he resembled his father, there was an Asian cast to his features, and Betsy suddenly recalled that Vern had brought a bride home from the Korean War. "What's up?" he asked, glancing at Betsy suspiciously.

"I dunno. This lady wants to ask me and you some

STOCKTON TWP PUBLIC LIBRARY
140 W. BENTON AVE.
STOCKTON, IL 61085

49

questions." He asked Betsy, "Are you doing another investigation?"

Jory said, "Oh, she's *that* lady!" He looked at her curiously, apparently having been told the story of the time Betsy had suspected Vern of murdering a vanished high-school sweetheart.

Vern said, "Yeah. I bet she's out to prove once and for all it was suicide, Paul killed his wife then hisself."

Jory retorted, "Or maybe she can prove it was Foster Johns murdered both of 'em." He smiled and leaned against the doorframe of the tiny office. "Sure, I'll answer any questions you have."

"Thank you. I understand you and your brother Alex were good friends with Paul."

"Sure. And with Foster Johns, too, back then. We all kind of hung out together."

"I never liked Paul Schmitt," growled Vern.

"Ah, you did too! You used to take us hunting and fishing."

"Maybe I did. But Paul was a strange kid, mean as a snake even with all his jokes."

Jory chuckled. "Remember that time he got hold of a little propane torch and would heat up a quarter and drop it on the sidewalk? Ow, ow, ow!" Jory laughed and shook his fingers as if they were burned.

Despite himself, Vern grinned, then drew up his sloping shoulders. "Yeah, but that time he scalded our cat, that wasn't funny."

Jory frowned. "That was an accident, he told you that, I told you that."

"I didn't think so. Neither did Alex."

"Aw, Alex! Who cares what he thinks?"

Vern shrugged. "Not me."

Betsy asked Jory, "How long have you known Paul Schmitt?"

"Since high school. He was a great guy, the funniest person I ever knew. He liked every kind of joke, and liked to play jokes on people."

"What can you tell me about his wife Angela?"

"I can tell you he murdered her," Vern cut in.

"You don't know that!" Jory said sharply. To Betsy he added, "He was nuts about her, totally nuts. He bought two cell phones and he was callin' her up all the time, asking her what she was doin'. An' he was always buying her things, a new dress, jewelry, flowers, fancy nightgowns. Then he'd call her three or four times to ask how she liked 'em, just so he could hear her thank him one more time. He'd say, 'Gotta keep 'em happy.'" Jory's smile faded. "He was real upset when she got shot. He looked so bad that when he was killed, the first thing I thought was that he killed himself. I said, 'I bet he killed himself,' didn't I?" He looked at his father.

Vern nodded, rugged face pulled into a heavy frown. "He took it hard, all right, but I don't agree that somebody else killing his wife would make him kill his own self. He wasn't the type. He was the type to kill her, and then kill hisself."

Jory shook his head, "It was proved he was beat up and shot by someone else."

Vern waved a thick, dirty hand dismissively. "Yeah, but who proved it? Mike Malloy, who couldn't prove corn flakes taste better with milk. Nah, I say he killed hisself and Malloy bungled it somehow. Maybe the gun fell behind the couch and Malloy couldn't find it, or it's even possible he had it and mislaid it, so he just said it was murder."

Betsy said, "Malloy isn't as stupid as all that—"

"Sure he is," said Vern. "Dumber than a box of rocks."

Jory said, "So what? It couldn't've been Paul, it had to be someone else; the same gun killed both of them. Paul wouldn't murder Angela, he was crazy about her."

Vern shifted his weight in his chair, settling in for an argument. "Same gun, sure—but it could've been Paul's gun. He had one, you know that."

"Then where is it?"

"I told you, Malloy lost it. And crazy is the right word. You said it yourself, he called her every five minutes when she wasn't at home, checking up on her. He liked her to stay at home, and he worked at home so he could be right there with her. He hated it when she took that job at the bookstore, so he took a job right down the street. They didn't need the money she brought in; I think she wanted out of the house because he was smothering her. Ten, eleven years they was married, and was like they'd gotten married last week. It wasn't love, it was more like he was obsessed. And he was getting worse, not better. He was always thinking she was having an affair, which it turned out she was, though where she found the time I don't know. But I don't blame her. So okay, he found out, and he shot her. I thought from the start he done it."

By the unheated tones of the argument, Betsy was sure this was an old, often-rehashed one.

Jory said, "Nope, you're wrong. Once Foster Johns admitted he and Angela were messing around, I knew it was Foster who killed her. Why the hell our police couldn't prove something as open and shut as that, I don't know."

Vern shook his head. "If Foster was in love with Angela, why in hell would he kill her?"

"Lover's quarrel. Or because she wanted to break it off. One or the other, plain as the nose on your face."

"The only thing plain—" began Vern.

Betsy intervened. "All right, all right. I understand you two don't agree. But suppose it wasn't suicide, and it wasn't Foster who killed Paul, either. Do you have any idea who else might have wanted him dead?"

"Don't you say it!" Vern said suddenly to his son, who had opened his mouth.

Jory obediently didn't say it. Instead he said, faux innocently, "What were you thinking I'd say, Dad?"

"You know what I'm talking about, and I won't have it said in my presence, I don't care if you are my son." His glare intensified. "Blood's thicker than water, no matter what he's done."

"Are you talking about Alex?" she asked.

"I never said a word, and I won't," said Jory, his expression truculent. "Anyhow, it was Foster. I knew all along it was Foster."

"Please don't say things like that when I'm in the same room with you," said Vern. "One of these days you'll say that and the roof will fall in on you, an' it

53

might take me along, too. You told me yourself right after Angela's murder that you thought Paul did it, and you even predicted Paul would either be arrested or kill hisself in the next couple days. You said it happens all the time, men killing their women, then themselves."

"I did not—"

"Dammit, yes, you did!"

"Well, all right, maybe I did, but just at first. Then we found out what really happened, only the cops couldn't prove it, and we end up living in a town where a murderer walks the streets!" Jory threw a disgusted look at his father, a half-shamed look at Betsy, and walked out.

5

The Monday Bunch was again in session. The weather had warmed enough to rain, but gale-force winds made it rattle against the front window of Crewel World like hail. "Raincoats and umbrellas for the trick-or-treaters this year," noted Martha.

"If they go out trick-or-treating at all," said Bershada. "My grandkids haven't since they were toddlers, and then it was just going around inside the apartment building they lived in."

It was Halloween. In honor of the holiday, Betsy had made a five-gallon urn of hot spiced cider for her customers, and all five members present had a steaming cup in front of them. Despite the holiday—or perhaps because of it—every one of them was working on a Christmas project. But the talk was of Halloweens past, when children in homemade costumes went door-to-door soliciting candy. "I remember one year when my brother, who always dressed as a tramp, came home with a pillowcase nearly full of candy," said Comfort. "Mother made him take most of it to the children's hospital in St. Paul, and he still had enough left to give himself three or four stomachaches." She was knitting a child's sweater dappled with snowmen, a gift for a great-grandchild.

"My father used to say that when he was a boy, they pulled awful pranks, soaping windows and tipping over outhouses," said Martha, who was working on Holiday House, a complex work in two pieces. One, lying finished on the table, was the front of a two-story house done in Hardanger and other fancy white-on-white stitches. The second had an elaborately-decorated Christmas tree down low and a lit candle up high; when the first piece was laid over it, the tree appeared in the living room window and the candle in an upstairs bedroom. She was working on the tree, using silks, metallics, and tiny beads. "Once, they dismantled a neighbor's Model A and reassembled it in the hayloft of his barn."

Alice said, "My brothers never thought up anything more imaginative than stealing the mayor's front gate."

Godwin, fashionable in a blue-and-maroon argyle sweater that set off his golden hair beautifully, said, "I always *loved* dressing up on Halloween." He was knitting a red-and-green scarf without looking, his fingers moving swiftly and economically. A tiny smile formed. "*Never* as a tramp, however."

Emily, her dark eyes focused on the Cold Hands, Warm Heart sampler she was cross-stitching, said, "Oh, I wish there were fancy dress balls nowadays, the really elaborate kind, where people come as Harlequin and Marie Antoinette and go dancing in a gigantic ball-room all lit with candles." She paused to complete a stitch. "But I've never even heard of someone holding one, much less been invited."

"You just don't move in the right circles, my dear," said Godwin. The ladies laughed. Godwin loved to hint at scandalous gay parties, but they were almost sure he'd never been to one in his life.

As on last Monday, Betsy yearned to sit down with them, but today she was stuck at her desk designing a new seasonal display. As soon as the store closed this evening, the cross-stitched black cats and jack-o'-lanterns would be cleared away to make room for a framed counted cross-stitch cornucopia, and a stand-up pillow shaped like a turkey. But there would be only a very few other acknowledgments of Thanksgiving— not with the retailers' most important holiday on the horizon: Christmas.

Her window and the major components of her seasonal display were due to go up tonight. Already she was behind other retailers, whose Christmas lights had begun to twinkle right after school started.

She glanced at the soft fabric sack under the table, three steps but many hours away. It held her Christmas stocking and a Ziploc bag of floss. If she was to get it to her finisher, she would have to work on it every night after the shop closed—and starting this weekend, the shop would be open all day Saturday and Sunday. That meant she couldn't go to Orchestra Hall Saturday night. She took a sip of hot spiced cider and sighed. She enjoyed stitching, and she enjoyed owning a needlework shop, but there never seemed to be enough time left over for anything else.

She looked down at her barely-started plan for the front window. Betsy kept a few needlepoint Christmas stockings out year round and, of course, Marilyn Leavitt Imblum's Celtic Christmas hung with the counted cross-stitch models year round. But there were other big, complex Christmas patterns it took cross-stitchers months to finish. They needed prodding to remind them to buy these projects in March, when everyone else was thinking about tulips and Easter bunnies. Betsy envied Cross Stitch Corner in Chicago, a shop with enough floor space to have a big, year-round Christmas display. As it was, her customers who bought the big ones now would display them next Christmas.

She studied her list of Christmas patterns in stock, her list of finished models, and her floor plan. She hadn't owned Crewel World very long, and while she was more sophisticated than when she began, she was still feeling her way into the retail stitchery business. Learning on this job was a dangerous undertaking; if it weren't for her other sources of income, Crewel World would have gone under months ago. And she knew she'd be much further along if she hadn't also encumbered herself with ownership of the building her shop was in, with its own numerous demands.

And weren't so often sidetracked by crime.

Interesting at this stage of her life—Betsy was in her middle fifties—to discover a heretofore latent talent for sleuthing. But once uncovered, it proved a powerful draw, eating up time she would otherwise have devoted to ordering stock, paying bills, record keeping, tax planning, salesmanship, and home improvement.

And designing her displays.

She looked over the assortment of patterns and models, and was satisfied with the plentitude and variety. Now, which was to go in the big front window to catch the eye of potential customers? She had already used a ruler to make a rectangle scaled to her window's dimensions, and had cut some blue scrap paper into rough shapes scaled to represent the items she thought should go in the window—too many, of course.

This scrap represented a spectacular, hand-painted needlepoint Christmas stocking, very eye-catching—but there was only the one, so if it sold at once, it would make a hole in the display. She put its paper shape aside. Maybe she should put up one of the knitted stockings instead? But which, the one knitted in bright Christmas colors? Or the one knitted in Scandinavian blue and white? Or the buff one knitted in fancy stitches, like an aran sweater? Not all three, that might make passersby think this was primarily a knitting supplies shop, which it wasn't, and also wouldn't leave room for the beautiful and complicated Teresa Wentzler Holly and Ivy sampler Sherry had begun for Betsy's predecessor and only finished a week ago. Betsy also had a nice collection of counted cross-stitch stockings. Maybe her window could be all stockings, knit, cross-stitched and needlepointed. Yes!

No. She'd already decided there must be a place for Just Nan's Liberty Angel, the one done in red, white and blue with a star-spangled banner.

There was the large and magnificent Marbek Nativity, but that would go in the back, on a low table against the wall, looking out through the opening between the tall set of box shelves that divided the counted cross-stitch area from the front of the shop. She would arrange one of the ceiling spots to shine directly on the big, glittery figures, so customers in front would feel as if they were looking into the Stable.

She pulled her attention from the back of the shop to the window. She'd put some of those small, adorable, *affordable* needlepoint canvases of Santas and rocking horses and alphabet blocks that could be finished quickly even by beginning stitchers. And she'd better save a corner for an announcement of January classes that needlepoint and knitting customers should sign up for.

And, of course, there were the fairy lights that would frame the window—she sketched some loops to indicate the space they'd take.

Already the window was looking overcrowded. Hmmm, if she took out two of the inexpensive canvases, and moved this stocking over here, and then this counted piece could go . . .

Her sketching was interrupted by the *Bing!* of the front door. Betsy looked up to see Mrs. Chesterfield coming in, and went at once to greet her. Mrs. Chesterfield was a good customer, but she could not pick a skein of wool from a basket without spilling all the contents, or pull a pattern from a rack without tipping it over. Equally bad, she often stepped on whatever fell near her feet.

"May I help you find something, Mrs. Chesterfield?" Betsy had decided that the next time Mrs. Chesterfield came in, she would follow her around, trying to keep her from bumping into racks and picking things up she knocked over before they got stepped on.

"I'm looking for a sampler pattern. But I don't know who it's by."

Mrs. Chesterfield went into the back room of the shop, where the counted cross-stitch patterns lived, and was reaching for a book on samplers when the rack behind her tipped over. Betsy was almost sure the woman's hip had bumped it and sent it rolling crookedly across the floor, shedding Water Colors floss as it went.

"I'll get it, it's all right," said Betsy. "You go ahead with your selection." She stooped to gather the beautiful pastel skeins.

Perhaps because she was concentrating on that task, she didn't see how Mrs. Chesterfield managed to pull a book from the middle shelf and at the same time cause half of the pretty display of clear glass "ort collectors" on an upper shelf to tumble to the floor. She must have reached up to brace herself—Mrs. Chesterfield was a bit arthritic.

"Watch where you're stepping!" said Betsy more sharply than she meant to, as one of the ornaments crumbled under Mrs. Chesterfield's heel.

"Well, where did those come from?" asked Mrs. Chesterfield, looking about her as she moved away from the shelves. "Honestly, Betsy, you should be more careful how you set up your displays. Every time I come in here, something gets broken."

"I know, it's awful," said Betsy, frowning because that was true. "I'll try to do better in future," she promised. "Here, why don't you sit at this table and look at your book. I'll bring you some more so you can see which one you like best. And would you like a cup of hot cider?"

"Why, thank you, Betsy, that would be lovely. Do you still have that tea-dyed linen in thirty-six–thirty-eight count? The pattern I'm looking for is an old one. I think it has a Tree of Life on it." Women who did samplers often found that to do an exact replica of very old patterns, they needed linen woven, like the antique original, with fewer strands per inch in one direction than the other. Thank God for Norden Crafts, which not only had such linen, but could supply it in a number of colors and counts.

Betsy said, "Yes, I have that. What size piece will you need?" Betsy selected three books on samplers and brought them to Mrs. Chesterfield. "Here you are."

"I won't know until I find the pattern. I know it's in

one of these books, Margaret told me about it."

Betsy didn't do samplers, so she couldn't help look. She brought a Styrofoam cup of cider to Mrs. Chesterfield, and on seeing she was securely seated in the chair, went back to her desk.

She had barely taken her seat when there was a soft crash from the back, its exact location hidden by one of the twin walls of box shelves that made a separate room of the back of the shop. Before Betsy could move, Godwin, winking and grinning at Betsy, was through the opening. Mrs. Chesterfield was heard to say, "How did that happen?"

And Godwin to reply, "It's just a few magazines, Mrs. Chesterfield. Nothing to worry about." His tone was very dry, pitched to reach Betsy's ears.

"I told you so," said Martha to Alice, and to Comfort, "What's she doing?"

"Told her what?" asked Betsy.

"Godwin says Mrs. Chesterfield has a poltergeist," said Comfort. "And Martha agrees with him." She was leaning back in her seat, trying to see what was going on. "Looks to me like she's sitting down."

"If Godwin is as bright as he seems, he'll make sure she stays in that chair."

Emily giggled. "Do you all really believe Mrs. Chesterfield is haunted?"

"I don't," said Alice, but quietly. Last Monday she had disagreed that Foster Johns was a murderer; she didn't like being the one who always disagreed. "No such thing," she added, and checked the count on the bright blue mitten she was knitting with an air indi-

62

cating she would say no more, and continued working down the palm.

There was another crash, this one louder. Emily stood and went to the entryway between the box shelves.

"Oh, my goodness, look at that!" she said.

"What?" asked Betsy, standing and leaning forward for a look. "Oh, no, that rack of scissors!"

"I've got it, you all stay out of here," said Godwin. He could be heard adding to Mrs. Chesterfield, "Please sit down again; I'll bring you whatever you want."

Emily and Betsy went back to their respective seats, too, and Emily said in a low voice, "Did you see how Mrs. Chesterfield was nowhere near that rack?"

"She never is," said Martha, rolling her gaze around the table.

"She moved away when it fell, of course," said Alice in a barely audible voice.

"Of course she did," agreed Betsy firmly, hoping to quash the gossip, and annoyed with Godwin for spreading it.

"Well, this is interesting," said Comfort, looking around the table, her knitting forgotten. "Do you mean to tell me that some of you believe in ghosts?"

"I don't," said Alice.

"Anyway, it's not a ghost, it's a poltergeist," said young Emily. She picked up her sampler. "And whether or not anyone believes it, Mrs. Chesterfield is haunted."

"What's a poltergeist?" asked Comfort.

"It's a mischievous spirit that throws things and

breaks things and moves things," explained Martha. "It tends to hang around a particular individual, usually an adolescent."

"Mrs. Chesterfield is hardly an adolescent," noted Alice.

"Only *usually* an adolescent," underlined Martha. "And usually these things happen only in their homes. But Mrs. Chesterfield's poltergeist isn't active in her home at all; instead, it follows her everywhere. It doesn't always 'act out,' but obviously today it is very active."

"Why, because it's Halloween?" asked Comfort.

"Could be," agreed Martha. "But I remember one Fourth of July when all the fireworks went off at once, scaring the men getting ready to fire them half to death, and there she was, sitting on the beach watching."

"How can you think that was her fault?" asked Alice with a snort. "My dear friend Mary Kuhfeld was in Philadelphia for the weeklong bicentennial celebration in 1976, and the night of July third all the fireworks on a pier went off at once, some coming right at the people standing on the shore. Do you think Mary is haunted by a poltergeist? Of course not. It was an accident. A worker dropped his flare, which started a fire and that's what set them all off. The same thing happened here that Fourth."

"Wouldn't surprise me to learn Mrs. Chesterfield was in Philadelphia that night, watching while her poltergeist tripped fireworks technicians," said Martha, but not seriously. The others chuckled.

Alice said, "You shouldn't say things like that. Some

people will take you seriously, and they'll start thinking there's no such thing as accident or even coincidence." She raised a defiant hand and snapped her fingers. "Poltergeists—hah!"

A huge black web fell out of the ceiling, wrapping her hand, her head, her shoulders.

Bershada screamed, Emily shrieked. Struggling to get free, Alice fell backward out of her chair.

"Here, here, here!" Betsy yelled, running around the table to stoop beside Alice. "Stop pulling at it, please!"

"Get it off me!" shouted Alice.

"What, what?" called Godwin, rushing out from behind the shelves.

"It's all right, it's all right!" cried Betsy, trying to hold Alice's hands still through the webbing. "Lie still, please, Alice!"

"What *is* it?" cried Alice, trying to obey and at the same time shrink from the horrible thing.

"It's a shawl," said Betsy.

"Why, of course!" said Comfort. "It was hanging from the ceiling," she explained from her place well away from the table, holding the tiny, half-knitted sweater to her breast like a shield. She took a step forward, her expression swiftly changing from frightened to amused.

"Oh? Oh!" Alice suddenly relaxed. "That's all it is?"

"Are you hurt, Alice?" asked Martha, coming out from behind a spinner rack of knitting accessories.

"I—I don't think so. But I'm afraid I may have torn this, Betsy."

"Yes, it is torn, a little." Betsy's face was twisted

with dismay. There was a substantial tear near one edge.

"Well, what was it doing up on the ceiling, anyway?" demanded Bershada, lifting her glasses and looking up.

"It's a display method, that's all," said Godwin. The other women also looked up at the several shawls hanging on the ceiling.

"Oh, why, so it is," said Bershada. "Clever."

"Not *that* clever," said Betsy sadly. Seeking more display space, she had taken to hanging some of her lighter models from slender threads attached to the soft tiles of her shop's ceiling with pins. None had ever broken loose before. On the other hand, this was the largest item she had ever attempted to suspend.

"Three Kittens uses plastic hooks that fasten to the metal strips of their acoustic ceiling," said Martha, naming a yarn shop in St. Paul.

"Where do they get them, I wonder?" said Betsy. "No, don't try to get up yet, Alice."

"Here, let me help," said Godwin, stooping across from Betsy.

"What's going on?" asked a new voice, and Mrs. Chesterfield came out from the back. "Is someone hurt?"

"No, but that beautiful Russian-lace shawl Betsy had hanging from the ceiling fell onto Alice's head," said Martha.

"Well, how on earth did that happen?" asked Mrs. Chesterfield.

"I think it was your polter—" said Godwin.

"Don't you say it!" she said, turning on him. "I won't listen to any more talk of me and a poltergeist!"

"No, of course not," said Betsy. "Goddy's just being silly. Aren't you, Godwin?"

"All right," he agreed, but with a smirk.

Mrs. Chesterfield looked at him suspiciously, but he instantly switched to his famous faux innocent look, complete with batting eyelashes and, barely mollified, she went back to the sampler books.

Godwin and Betsy continued disentangling Alice from the large black shawl, and in the silence there came a muffled choking sound. It was Emily, trying to stifle a giggle.

"Hush, Emily," said Martha. "Alice has received a terrible fright."

"Th-that's true," giggled Emily. "It scared all of us. Did you see the way we all shot out of our chairs when that shawl fell?" She giggled some more.

Bershada said with a significant smile, "That will teach Alice to say 'hah' to poltergeists."

"Come on, both of you!" said Betsy. "Didn't you ever hear of coincidence?"

Bershada said, "Coincidence? Mmmmm-hmmmm!"

Emily giggled from behind both hands held over her nose and mouth.

Godwin asked Alice, "Well, if it wasn't the you-know-what, how in the world did it manage to tear loose?" He glanced up at the ceiling, which was about nine feet high. Alice was a tall woman, but her reach wasn't *that* high.

"I didn't touch the thing!" said Alice crossly, trying

to hold still as the last strands of fine black yarn were unwound from her earrings. "Ouch, please be careful! I was just sitting there when it fell on me with no warning! Now help me—Oof!" She grunted as Godwin helped her to her feet.

"Are you all right?" asked Betsy.

"I think so. But oh, all my joints are shaken loose! Thank you, Godwin."

"Is it repairable?" asked Comfort, watching Betsy look at the tear. The shawl was a fragile, very difficult pattern of knit lace, a large but gossamer article Betsy had borrowed from a customer to interest advanced knitters in a book of patterns and the expensive wool it called for.

Betsy began to fold the shawl. "I'll see if Sandy can repair it." Sandy Mattson had more than once saved important pieces with her ability to invisibly repair them. At a price, of course. Betsy sighed, and took the shawl to the desk.

Godwin winked at the table and went between the box shelves to ask Mrs. Chesterfield in a high voice, "Have you decided which book you want, Mrs. Chesterfield?"

"Goddy," warned Betsy.

"We're fine, aren't we, Mrs. Chesterfield? Of course we are. Now, how about this one?" His tone was obediently subdued, and only lightly cordial.

"Yes, I think so. Thank you, Godwin. And I want a fat quarter of the uneven weave linen. If you don't have it in tea-dyed, then unbleached."

"Yes, ma'am."

The women stitched in silence until Mrs. Chesterfield paid for her book and linen, and left.

Alice said, "I feel sorry for that poor woman."

"What's this?" said Martha. "I thought you didn't believe in poltergeists."

"I don't," she replied, lifting her strong chin in a stubborn gesture. "But her life in the last few years has become a series of sad coincidences. I wonder if she has come to believe in the poltergeist herself—and how sad for her if she has."

6

L et's talk about something else," said Martha. "Something more cheerful."

Godwin, coming to sit down, said, "Well, it's Halloween, so let's tell ghost stories."

Comfort laughed. "Ghost stories are cheerful?"

Bershada said, "I just love ghost stories—the scarier, the better."

"Maybe we shouldn't go there," said Emily. "I think we just met a ghost. Alice, I know I was laughing, but when that shawl fell on you, that was authentically scary."

Alice said, "Even I was foolish, panicking like that. Why, you'd think I changed my mind about poltergeists, when of course I haven't. I was just startled."

"Mmmmmmm-hmmmmh," said Bershada. "Still, something like that is enough to turn all of us into medieval peasants, hanging wolfsbane on the door and wearing garlic around our necks, scared of every bump in the night."

"It's not night," said Emily, "it's broad daylight." She looked out the window at the rain-dark street. "Well, cloudy daylight. Look, someone's coming."

The door to the shop went *Bing!* and with an effort a woman in a wheelchair pushed herself over the threshold. She was an attractive woman of about thirty with short blond hair—currently plastered against one side of her face by rain—and brown eyes. She wore a red sweater and blue jeans under a yellow rain cape, which she pulled off and dropped on the floor near the door.

"Hi, Carol," said Betsy, coming to close the door for her. "Glad you could brave such terrible weather."

"Oh, wheeling around in the wind blows the cobwebs out of my head. I miss going to an office where there are live human beings and coffee breaks and football pools. Of course, one pleasure of working at home is that weekends become moveable feasts. I worked yesterday so I've declared today a Sunday." She stopped at the other end of the library table. "What are we talking about?"

"Ghost stories," said Alice, disapproval in her deep voice.

"Of course, what else on Halloween? Have I missed any juicy ones?"

"Not yet," said Bershada. "But we did have a little scare a few minutes ago." She explained about the shawl's fall onto Alice's head.

"Have mercy!" exclaimed Carol. "That must have

scared you out of ten years' growth, Alice."

"Not to mention the rest of us," said Godwin. "But Mrs. Chesterfield is gone, taking her poltergeist with her."

"Do you believe in poltergeists, Godwin?" asked Carol.

"No, of course not," he said, pretending to spit lightly to the left and right and making fake cabalistic signs with his right hand. "Do you?"

"No," she said, laughing, "but I have to believe in ghosts, since we have one living with us."

"Does he follow you around like Mrs. Chesterfield's poltergeist?" asked Bershada, looking past Carol for traces of ectoplasm.

"No, he stays at home." Carol made a little ceremony of getting out her project, a half-completed cross-stitch pattern of Santa standing sideways in a froth of fur and beard: Marilyn Leavitt-Imblum's Spirit of Christmas. These were all delaying tactics that allowed the tension to grow.

"Oh, all right, I'll break down and beg: Please, tell us all about it," said Godwin.

"She doesn't have to if she doesn't want to," objected Alice, still shaken from the episode of the shawl.

Emily seconded her. "Anyway, how can we be interested in ghost stories when we're all working on Christmas projects?"

Carol said, "Christmas is a very traditional time for ghost stories. Dickens's *A Christmas Carol* is a ghost story."

71

"Why, so it is," said Martha. "I never thought of that. So tell us about your ghost, Carol. "What does it do? Go bump in the night?"

"Once in a while, though it's more usually a sound like a marble rolling across the floor. But he's mostly a friendly ghost, except to carpenters and plumbers and electricians."

Betsy chuckled and asked from across the room, "What has he got against them? Their prices?"

"No, he doesn't want any changes made to the house. He's the original owner, my housemate's grandfather. His name is Cecil, he was a dentist. He and his wife bought the house back in the early 1920s as a summer vacation home—their other house was in Minneapolis."

Godwin jested, "How do you know that's who it is? Does he come into your bedroom and try to pull your teeth?"

Carol laughed back, but persisted, "I'm serious. Let me tell you the story. Cecil, his wife, and their four daughters all moved out to that house every summer to get away from the heat of the city."

Emily nodded. "My great-grandparents did the same thing, moved out here in the summer. Great-grandpop commuted every day on the streetcar steamboats."

Carol said, "This was a bit later, Cecil drove a car into town. But in the summer of 1935, when he was only forty-seven, Cecil had a heart attack. He survived it, but he became very worried about leaving his family without a man to take care of them. He tried to get well, but two years later he had another heart attack and died. The next summer, his widow and her daughters moved out of the city as usual, but started experiencing strange noises in the house. At first they didn't know what it was, but then they started getting an occasional whiff of pipe smoke. Cecil had loved his pipe."

"Ooooooooh," said Bershada, smiling.

"Go on, go on," urged Comfort.

Carol smiled. "Well, one by one the daughters married and moved away. The youngest daughter inherited the house when their mother died; and she and her husband decided to live there year round. She was Susan's mother. All this time, there were still these noises and sometimes the smell of pipe smoke. Nothing was ever broken, but she did notice the noises were worse when they'd do spring-cleaning, especially if they hung new drapes or painted. Like I said, he didn't like changes. Cecil would slam doors and stomp around upstairs until they were finished.

"Susan says she was aware of a presence in the house from her early childhood, and just accepted it as part of what it was like to live there. A few years ago her mother needed money, so Susan bought the house from her, but her mother still lives with us. She's an invalid now, the last of the four sisters. Susan says Grandfather Cecil is still watching over his last daughter, and will likely go when she dies."

"So this ghost story is only hearsay," said Alice. "You've never seen or heard anything."

"Oh, no, I've experienced him, too, door closings, footsteps, marble rollings, pipe tobacco, and all. In fact, I am the cause of a really serious outbreak. You see, when Susan invited me to move in with her and her mother, they had to make some changes, real changes, building ramps and widening doorways and installing an elevator to the second floor. When things got under way, Cecil really went to work. Doors wouldn't stay closed—or open, footsteps went up and down the stairs all day long, and marbles rolled all night. Then the carpenter began complaining he'd misplaced a hammer or screwdriver, and the electrician couldn't keep track of his wires and switches. This was something new and we just thought they were careless. But then Cecil started to sabotage their cars. The carpenter knocked off work one day, and his car wouldn't start. He checked under the hood and fooled around with it, and finally he called a tow truck. And once the car arrived at the garage, it worked just fine. The first time this happened, we were thinking he ought to get a tune-up, but after it happened a few times, we knew: It was Cecil. We discussed it and finally agreed to tell the workmen what it was. The way they stared at us, I thought we'd have to find a new construction firm. I've never seen five pairs of eyes that big."

"Did they quit?"

"Oddly enough, no. They kind of dared each other, and it turned into one of those macho games. But it worked, they stuck with it, and finally got it done. I think they were even more relieved than we were by the time they finished up."

Bershada said, "Funny he doesn't aim any of that

stuff at you. I mean, doesn't Cecil realize you were the reason for all those big changes to 'his' house?"

"Well, I *am* grateful he didn't think I was an intruder and try to run me off," said Carol. "I wonder if perhaps he understands there's a bond between Susan and me. For example, just the other night we were finishing supper and I heard music coming from upstairs. 'What's that?' I asked. 'Do you hear that music?' Susan's mother got the funniest look on her face, and Susan went up to see what it was. It was a big old music box, the kind that plays when you open the lid. She brought it down to show us." Carol moved her hands to describe a box about fourteen by eight inches. "No one had touched it in years, but she walked into the kitchen with it still playing. You know the song, 'Two Sleepy People'?"

"*Sleepless in Seattle*!" exclaimed Emily. "That was one of the old songs from that movie."

"Yes, and that's what was playing on the music box. Susan's mother said Cecil loved that song and bought the music box as a present for his wife."

"Awwwww," said Emily. "That's kind of nice."

Martha agreed, "For a ghost story, it wasn't very scary."

"It scared the carpenters and the plumber. But I'm glad Cecil's only concern is that his remaining daughter is all right. He loved Susan's mother the best of his girls, and he's still concerned about her."

There was a little silence, then Comfort said, "I saw a ghost once."

"Tell us about it!" said Bershada.

75

"Well, remember when Paul and Angela Schmitt were murdered?"

"Oh, not that again!" said Martha. "We talked that to death last week, remember?"

"Did you?" said Carol. "I'm sorry I missed it. I would have told you how Angela and my sister Gretchen were best friends in high school."

"Did you know Angela?" asked Betsy alertly.

"Not really. But the day she was killed, Gretchen came over and cried for hours in our mother's kitchen. She was sure Paul had done it; that is, until he was shot two nights later."

Comfort said, "It was Paul's ghost I saw, and on the night he was shot."

"Really!?" exclaimed Carol. "What was he doing? Did he know you? Did he tell you who murdered him?"

"No, it wasn't like that, not as if he came especially to speak to me. You see, I was walking up Water Street from the Minnehaha ticket office—I volunteer there four days a week when the boat is running," she explained. "Anyway, it was near the end of the season and I'd stayed late to do some bookkeeping and restock the racks of sweatshirts, so it was after dark. The weather was pretty much like it is right now, wind and all, and there wasn't another soul on the street. I stopped in front of the bookstore to turn my umbrella right side out, and noticed they had replaced the broken front window. I stood there a minute because my eye was caught by the display of Jim Ogland's *Postcard History of Lake Minnetonka*. That book has such a nice cover. And then I saw someone in the store. A man."

"Was he all bloody and awful?" asked Bershada hopefully.

"No. Or at least it was so dark, I couldn't see much detail. The wind died down suddenly and my umbrella came to its senses, and then I saw someone move. At first I just thought someone was in the store, an employee. But then I realized there was only that dim light burning at the back, the one they turn on as they leave for the night, so then I wondered if I was seeing a burglary in progress."

"That would have been enough for me," declared Emily. "There are lots of things just as scary as ghosts, and burglars are one of them."

"You're right, and I should have run away, but I was so surprised, I just stood there, gaping. Suddenly, the man stooped down, and I thought he'd seen me, but then he straightened up again. I couldn't imagine what he was doing. It was dark in the store, and I wasn't even sure I was seeing someone. He was over beside the checkout counter, near the wall and halfway behind that rack where they keep the finger puppets, or used to. He moved, kind of glided, away from there and went behind that couch they have for browsers. He was standing sideways, and I could see his silhouette against the light, and suddenly I recognized Paul Schmitt. He was standing still, head down, like he was praying, or waiting for something. Then he turned away—and all of a sudden he was gone, like he melted into the shelves. I couldn't think what he was doing in there. I had been thinking, it's a burglar, I should go call the police, but I couldn't get my feet to move. Now I recognized Paul Schmitt, that nice man from church, not some unknown burglar. Then I thought about Angela, and I was embarrassed, like you get when you see someone doing something and he thinks no one is looking. I wondered if he wasn't paying a private visit to the scene of his wife's death.

"That made me feel embarrassed to stand there staring, so I got my feet back under control and walked away."

"You should have called the police," said Alice.

"And told them what? Any story I tried to tell them would sound ridiculous. I went on to the Lucky Wok and had some of their moo shi pork for dinner and then walked home."

"Weren't you scared to go home?" asked Godwin. "I mean, you live alone and all."

"No, not at all, because I didn't know it was a ghost I'd seen. I was tired and went to bed before the news, so it wasn't till the next morning I heard that he'd been found murdered in his house. And when I thought about it, it seemed to me that I saw him in the store right about the time that someone shot him."

"Ooooooooh," breathed Bershada, and they all looked thrilled down to their toes—except Alice, but she didn't say anything.

Emily said, "I suppose he went there to gather up his wife's spirit and take her with him to the afterlife."

"Well, I don't recall hearing any reports that Angela's ghost was seen in the bookstore," said

Comfort. "Do you?"

"Well . . . no," said Emily. "But that doesn't mean she wasn't there. Maybe she knew he was going to follow her into the spirit world and kind of hung around waiting for him."

"If I were Angela's ghost, I certainly wouldn't hang around hoping the ghost of my husband, who I doubt was going to heaven, would come and take me with him," declared Alice.

"Why wouldn't he go to heaven?" asked Godwin.

"Anyway, she certainly did," declared Martha. "She was such a sweet and good woman. Maybe he hoped she would put in a good word for him."

"That doesn't explain why she waited for him," said Bershada. "How did she know he was coming so soon?"

"We don't know everything about the afterlife," said Emily. "Maybe she did know."

That brought a little pause while they reflected on the mysteries of love and the afterlife.

"He did love her very much," said Godwin softly.

"I don't think he did," said Alice. "I think it was more like an obsession."

"I'd like someone to be obsessed with me," said Bershada. "Someone whose every thought is about my happiness."

"No, you don't," said Alice firmly. "It's not about your happiness, and it isn't nearly as pleasant as true love. And when someone dies, my understanding is that such things as human relationships are abandoned."

79

"Oh, I don't believe that!" said Godwin. "Surely true love would last through eternity! There are all kinds of stories about a ghost coming to the bedside of a husband or wife."

"Yes, Alice, how can you doubt such serious things as love and ghosts and the afterlife?" said Bershada.

"I'm not doubting the afterlife, which I believe in most firmly," said Alice. "But ghosts are stuff and nonsense."

"But all those stories!" reiterated Godwin. "There are fictional ghost stories, I know that, but there are true ghost stories, too. And Comfort is only telling you what she actually saw!"

"I think that when it's late at night and you're tired or hungry and already nervous because you're out in a thunderstorm, or you are all alone in an old house and perhaps have been reading spooky stories, naturally you may conclude an unusual noise, or a dance of headlights on the ceiling, or even your own reflection is a ghost."

Martha said, "You're right, of course, Alice. But how to explain what happened to me back when I was about eleven or twelve? It was the dead of winter and the middle of the night. My father used to turn the furnace down at night to save fuel, so it was very cold in the house. I had a thick quilt on the bed and was sound in a cozy sleep—until something bumped into the bed and woke me up. I thought it was the cat jumping up, and I waited for him to come up to the pillow purring like he usually did." She smiled. "There's nothing quite as friendly as a cat with cold feet. But it wasn't the cat, or at least he didn't come up to ask to be let under the covers. Then I heard a voice say, plain as day, 'Her eyes are open.' It was pitch dark in that room, there's no way anyone could have seen whether my eyes were open or closed."

"Cool!" said Carol. "Then what happened?"

"Nothing, I burrowed under the covers and didn't come up till morning."

There was a reflective pause. "It was probably your mother," said Alice, "checking to see if you were all right in the cold."

"No. It was a woman's voice, but definitely not my mother's. Anyway, like I said, no one could have seen if my eyes were open or not."

"Were they?" asked Emily.

"Of course. I told you, I woke up when something bumped my bed."

"Who do you think it was?" asked Carol.

"I have no idea. And I never heard them again."

" 'Them'?" said Betsy. "How do you know there was more than one?"

"Well, she wasn't talking *to* me, she was talking *about* me. So that meant at least one other . . . person was present."

"Ooooooooh," said Bershada, moving her shoulders to dislodge a delicious shiver.

Godwin said maliciously, "How do you explain that, Alice?"

Alice shrugged. "A dream, obviously."

"It wasn't a dream," said Martha. "I was wide awake, I'd been wakened by the bump. But there also weren't any weird lights or footsteps or a chill breeze, or any of the usual stuff of ghost stories. And it wasn't my father, either," she said with a little sniff, forestalling Godwin's next sly suggestion.

So instead Godwin said, "How about you, Bershada? Do you have a ghost story?"

"Well, actually, I do. Only mine's different from Martha's, I didn't know it was a ghost. I thought it was an usher."

"At a *wedding?*" said Martha, scandalized.

"No, no," said Bershada, laughing. "At the Guthrie!"

"Oh, *him!*" said Godwin. "You saw Richard Miller!"

"Yes, that's the name. Have you seen him, too?"

"No, but I've heard about him. When did you see him?"

"Oh, this was years ago. My husband's parents took Mac and me to see *Amadeus*, and this usher kept walking up and down the aisle, blocking our view. The ushers are supposed to go out to the lobby during a performance, so it was annoying. He didn't seem to be looking for someone in particular, like you'd expect if it was an emergency or something. And he didn't seem interested in the play, either. He was just kind of observing the audience. I could see he was young, maybe only in his late teens, and he had a big mole on one cheek, very noticeable. I knew he was an usher because he had the sports coat they wear, with the insignia on the pocket?" She made a gesture over her left breast. "So during the intermission we complained to one of the other ushers, and he laughed and said we'd seen Richard Miller, who was an usher back in

82

the sixties who committed suicide."

"How did this usher kill himself?" asked Betsy. "Hang himself from a balcony rail?"

"Betsy!" said Emily.

"He didn't kill himself in the theater at all," said Godwin. "He did it in the Sears parking lot on Lake Street."

"That old place?" said Bershada. She explained to Betsy, "It's closed now, has been for a long, long time, but the building is still there, and the parking lot. It's a big building, very nice-looking in that art-deco way. They keep talking about doing something with it, but haven't so far. Anyway, you'd think he'd haunt that building."

"Maybe he does," said Martha. "Only there's nobody around to see him."

"Or he haunts the parking lot," said Comfort. "I can just hear the warnings: 'Don't park in row three, slot nineteen, or you'll come back to find a see-through stranger in your backseat.'"

Emily giggled uncomfortably, but Alice cleared her throat in a disparaging way.

Godwin said, "Instead, for some reason, he came back to the Guthrie and he gets in the way of customers." He frowned and said, "Maybe that's what Paul Schmitt was doing, not haunting the house he died in, but a place where something sad happened."

"Or a place where he did something wicked," said Carol.

"What do you mean?" asked Martha.

"Well, suppose he found out about Angela and

83

Foster and murdered Angela. True love can turn to hate in a wink of an eye, you know. I remember wondering right after Angela was murdered if maybe Paul hadn't done it."

Godwin objected, "Well, if that's a cause for haunting, you'd think Paul would haunt Foster Johns's office. After all, Foster murdered Paul."

Alice said, "Nobody knows that for sure. Everyone's been saying how nice Paul was. Well, suppose he wasn't nice, despite his smiles. Suppose someone were to get serious about looking into his and Angela's deaths." She raised an eyebrow at Betsy. "I think it's possible there might be other suspects."

"You shouldn't speak ill of the dead," said Bershada with a frown.

"You shouldn't make saints of people who don't deserve it!" said Alice. "If Martha is right and Paul was a jealous man, and it is not at all uncommon for that emotion to accompany obsession—or 'true love,' as you will have it—then he would have been upset about any man who talked with his wife. So you can imagine how painful it was for him to think of her in that book-store, where men came in every day. I think he was a brother to those dreadful Taliban people who made their women cover themselves with—what was it called? That sack thing. He would have loved it if America adopted Taliban customs for women, and made Angela wear that sack thing and never go any-where without him along."

Emily said, "I'd like to see them try to put the women of America into burkas!"

Martha snickered. "And how could they get American men back to the twelfth century? Make them all ride donkeys to work?"

The mental picture of a big herd of donkeys laden with men in business suits trekking down 35W and 394 into Minneapolis, talking on their cell phones and batting their unfortunate mounts on the rumps with their briefcases, caused everyone to stop and smile for a few moments.

Then Godwin said, "I've never seen a ghost, but my grandmother heard one. She was baking Thanksgiving pies one morning when she heard, plain as day, her sister Frankie saying, 'Milly, call an ambulance! I fell and broke my ankle! Help, Milly!' What was weird is that Great-aunt Frances was in Columbus, Ohio, at the time, and Grandmama lived in St. Paul. Grandmama was so sure she'd heard her sister asking for help that she called the police in Columbus and insisted they go to Frankie's house. Sure enough, she'd fallen on a patch of ice in the backyard and would have laid there until her husband came home from work, and as it wasn't even noon yet, likely he'd have found her frozen to death."

Martha said, "That's not a ghost story. Your great-aunt wasn't dead."

"Well, okay, I guess it isn't. But it's a paranormal story." He looked at Alice. "Explain that, if you can."

Alice obediently tried. "I suppose she was thinking about her sister and imagined she heard her voice. Or perhaps . . . perhaps Frankie prayed very hard for rescue and a miracle happened. God allowed her cry for help to reach Milly's ears."

"He works in mysterious ways," agreed Bershada. "Or perhaps Godwin had just made that up, another way to pick on Alice. Shame on you, Goddy!"

"This *is* a true story," said Godwin, hurt. "It was written up in the *Columbus Dispatch*. You *have* to believe it, Bershada, I believed *you* about Richard Miller. I've been there *lots* of times, and I know *all about* him, but I've never *seen* him. Now they're tearing down the old theater, I probably never will. Unless—do you think he'll go haunt the new building?"

Bershada said, "Can they do that sort of thing?"

Carol said, "There is supposed to be a family in the United States who are direct descendants of a duke, and they had a family ghost from the twelfth century follow them over here. One of those kind that when she appears, there's a death in the family."

Emily said, "I know a story like that."

"What, about someone who saw Richard Miller's ghost and died?" asked Godwin.

"No, mine is about the Wendigo."

Everyone at the table smiled but Betsy. "What's the Wendigo?" she asked.

"He's a really old spirit, the Indians told the white settlers about him," said Godwin.

"Oh, no, it isn't a spirit," said Carol, surprised at him. "The Wendigo is a big, hairy creature, sort of like Bigfoot, who finds Indians alone in the forest and eats them."

"Ish!" said Bershada.

Godwin said, "*Eats* them? Like a *cannibal?* I didn't know that."

Betsy said, "It's not cannibalism to eat something other than your own kind."

"*Anyway,*" said Emily, to regather their attention. "The Wendigo is like nine or ten feet tall, and covered with gray fur. And it has a bright light shining in its forehead. Early settlers saw it, and pretty soon they realized there was a death in the family of whoever saw it, that's why what Carol said about the duke's ghost reminded me. It's still around, people still see the Wendigo, only now mostly just up north. And when they do, someone dies."

Godwin said, "*That's* your scary story?"

Emily said, "No, that's just the explaining part. My great-grandmother saw it. She and her second husband were up on the Iron Range, on the road between Eveleth and Virginia—he was a surveyor, and she was his assistant—and she told my mother, who told me, that they were walking back from a job. It was getting dark, and there were trees along one side of the road, and she saw this light-colored thing back in there, and first she thought it was the trunk of a birch growing alone among the pines, and then that it was a light-colored bear standing on its hind legs. Only it was too tall to be a bear. It turned toward them, and she saw it had a light shining out of its forehead, and she knew what it was. She screamed 'Wendigo!' and they both ran all the way back into Eveleth. Almost two miles it was, and they never stopped once. And Ralph—that was her second husband—he died two days later of a heart attack."

"And we mustn't think that perhaps running scared in near-darkness for two miles might have been the cause of that," said Alice very dryly.

"Did her husband know about the legend of the Wendigo, that it means a death?" asked Betsy.

"Oh, yes, they both did, and they wondered who it was going to be. Great-grandmother called all her children the next day to see if they were all right, and they were, so she was starting to think it was a mistake when Ralph collapsed at the supper table and died. Great-grandmother had thought it might be she herself who was doomed, but it never occurred to her it would be her husband, because he was five years younger than her, and he didn't have any medical problems."

Betsy asked, "Do all of you believe in the Wendigo?"

"I don't, of course," said Alice.

Godwin said, "I understand you don't have to believe in the Wendigo for him to appear to you." There was a blank silence, then everyone laughed, even Alice.

7

When Betsy climbed the stairs to her apartment that night, she was exhausted. Sophie, anxious and whining, trotted ahead and led the way into the kitchen. Betsy opened the cabinet under the sink and gave her cat the little scoop of Iams Less Active that was dinner. It was not possible the vastly overweight animal was hungry—Sophie snacked all day long: potato chips, fragments of cookies and the occasional mayonnaise-soaked corner of lettuce, all cadged from customers down in the shop.

Betsy had tried to institute a policy of no food or drink in the shop, and failing that, of not feeding samples of it to the cat. When that also failed, she pretended it wasn't happening. Sophie held up her end by pretending to be famished in the evenings. So not just in the morning but also in the evening the cat was served a small low-calorie, high-protein meal that at least filled in the vitamin gaps her otherwise poor diet offered.

Betsy was too tired to even think of cooking for herself. She was searching her larder for a can of tuna when the phone rang. She thought about letting her machine catch it, but the receiver was in easy reach, so she picked it up.

"Hello," she said.

"Oh, my dear, are you as tired as you sound?"

drawled a friendly voice.

"Gosh, yes, totally bushed. Hi, Morrie, I'm glad to hear your voice, but I hope you aren't thinking to take me somewhere tonight."

"When you check your machine, you'll find I've been calling you all evening. But it's too late now to go trick-or-treating, we've missed the start of the special showing of *Abbott and Costello Meet the Wolfman*, and the costume party has reached the stage where only people with at least three drinks under their belts are having any fun. Where have you been?"

"Down in the shop. We did our Christmas window tonight."

"Ah, you're one of those merchants who starts in right after Halloween."

"That's right, I'm very conservative, unlike those who begin in September. Still, by the time Christmas Eve rolls around, I'm going to be totally sick of Christmas patterns, Christmas wrap, yarn in Christmas colors, and angels with wings done in Wisper and gold metallic. But by gum, the shop is going to be in the black."

Morrie laughed. He had a good laugh, frequently used, and she could picture him, head thrown back and mouth wide open. He was a tall, thin man in his early sixties, with not quite enough silver hair, a lantern jaw, and ears that stuck out. But he had the kindest eyes and sweetest demeanor Betsy had encountered in a long, long while. He was wonderful to have around, because with quiet ardor he had taken charge of making her life enjoyable. "Have you had supper yet?" he asked.

"I was about to open a can of tuna. I can make it into a salad if you want a share."

"Put that can opener away right now. I'll be there in half an hour with—what shall I bring, a pizza?"

"Bless you. Thanks."

Ninety minutes later, over the last slices of now-cold pizza, they were talking about—what else?—ghost stories.

"Do you believe in ghosts?" he asked.

"Well, I saw a ghost once, so I guess I have to."

He was amused. "Where did you see a ghost?"

"In that most traditional of places: a cemetery. I was standing in one of those little country ones, the kind a family would put up for itself back in the pioneer days. I was reading epitaphs—don't you just love old epitaphs?"

"'A coffin, sheet, and grave's my earthly store; 'tis all I want, and kings can have no more,'" he recited in an oratorical voice.

"Oh, that's a nice one! Did you read that on a tombstone?"

"No, in a book I got as a Christmas present a long time ago. It's called *Over Their Dead Bodies*, which has to be one of the cleverest titles ever dreamed up. But you were in this cemetery at midnight and a ghost swirled up out of a grave and said to you . . ." he prompted.

"No, it wasn't anything like that. I was in this little cemetery, but it was a sunny afternoon, and my sister Margot said, 'Hey, look at this one!' and I turned to look, and as my eyes went past the woodlot that was the

91

border of the cemetery, suddenly it wasn't a woodlot, but an open field of grass and a woman in a long white dress was standing there with a child in a shorter white dress and one or the other of them had a parasol. I was just so surprised, I looked again and it was the woodlot again."

"Can it be a ghost if it's a whole landscape?" Morrie asked.

"I don't know. I only know what I saw, for just an instant."

"What were they doing, the woman and child? Did they see you?"

"No, they were looking down at something in the grass. It wasn't scary or anything, it was just a glimpse of a long-ago time, that piece of ground reciting a lesson it had learned. Or that's my theory, anyhow."

"Are you sure you didn't imagine it?"

"Yes, because I was about twelve and if I ever thought of the parade of fashion, which I didn't very much, I would have assumed that somehow we jumped from huge skirts, like during the Civil War, to the flapper's fringed little dress, like during the Roaring Twenties. But this woman was wearing something long and soft with no hoops. Her dress was like gauze, several layers of gauze. I found out later that material is called 'lawn.' She had a ruffle somewhere on the bodice, I think. And not leg-o'-mutton sleeves, but long ones."

"What was her hairstyle?"

"I don't remember. She was holding the child's hand. They were happy, I think."

She took a sip of wine, and let it rest on her tongue a moment before swallowing it. Morrie's taste in adult beverages was much like hers, not highly sophisticated—the bottle had a picture of a toad in a vest on it—but well beyond soda-sweet stuff.

"Do you know what the temperature was in Fort Myers today?" he asked.

"No, what?"

"Seventy-eight. You'll love it down there. How much vacation do you get every year?"

"None. I'm the owner, I don't get a vacation."

"Nonsense. You have to take at least a week off in, say, February or March."

Morrie was being forced to retire—well, not entirely forced, he knew it was coming and in fact was ready for it. He had bought a house in a Fort Myers gated community five years ago, furnished it, spent two weeks there every winter and rented it out the rest of the year. He was planning to move down there permanently when he retired early next year.

Then he'd met Betsy. It was during a course of a homicide investigation—where else?—and there had been an immediate attraction. He'd found her clever and lucky, and she thought him charming and intelligent. But while in a few months he was ready to commit to a relationship, she was unwilling to relocate to Florida.

He thought she was crazy to want to stay in the frigid north; she thought he was crazy to abandon a lifetime's worth of friends. Neither was seeing anyone else, but he couldn't persuade her to sell the shop and she couldn't persuade him to stay in Minnesota.

"Why do you think I should take a vacation in March?" she asked now.

"Because by then you'll be really sick of winter—and I'll really be missing you." He lifted her pepperoni-scented fingers and kissed them.

Betsy came down to the shop a little heavy-eyed the next morning. She had let Morrie stay a little later than she should have, and her only satisfaction was that he had to be at work by nine, while her shop didn't open until ten. She went down around quarter to, Sophie happily trundling ahead of her.

In the shop, Betsy looked around with satisfaction. There was a little artificial Christmas tree on the checkout desk, waiting for customers to decorate it with stitched ornaments. Her own ornament, a white cat with a wreath around its neck, stitched on maroon Aida cloth from a Bucilla kit, already hung on a branch. The tree would be given to someone in town who otherwise wouldn't have one. Betsy's sister, who had founded Crewel World, had begun the custom, and Betsy was pleased to keep it up.

The Marbek Nativity glowed under the track light, and on the wall behind it were three counted cross stitch stockings, Marilyn Leavitt-Imblum's Angel of the Morning, Dennis P. Lewan's scene of snow-covered Victorian houses at sunset, a Christmas sampler from Homespun Elegance, and a cross-stitch pattern of Santa aloft in his sleigh with an American flag flying off the back of it.

For the less sentimental, there was an amusing model of Linda Connors's black cat destroying a Christmas tree.

For the curmudgeons, there was Santa sitting on a chimney, pants down, a satisfied scowl on his face, and under it the legend, "For Those Who Have Been *Really* Naughty . . . ."

But Betsy was most concerned about the front window. She went out to take a look at it in the daylight. Last night she had thrown out her plan for a Christmas theme, having been overcome by a wonderful, exciting *Idea*. But what if the Idea had been a bad one? After all, she'd been tired. Or if it had been a good one, perhaps she'd done it too fast, and now, in the chill light of morning it looked slipshod. She hadn't sat down and drawn up a plan, after all. She and Godwin, laughing with excitement, had just pulled patterns and models and stuck them up quickly, like children drawing on a wall. (How great it was to have an employee like Godwin!) But what if the window was just a muddle?

She stood a moment, eyes closed, outdoors in front of the window. Then opened them.

It wasn't awful, or slipshod. It was good. The theme was the onset of winter, which every culture that ever lived in four seasons has marked. The layout was terrific—not too cluttered, not too regimented. The eye moved naturally from place to place.

There was a knit stocking with its pattern of Christmas tree lights, and Just Nan's Liberty Angel, and the needlepoint rocking horse, but there was also a canvas that, when finished and cut out, could be sewn up into a set of Hanukkah dreidels. And there was a Wiccan pattern of Bertcha, goddess of the winter solstice. There was the Kwanzaa kinora with its black, red, and green candles, stitched in silks. There was a canvas of Arabic calligraphy, to be covered with gold and silver stitches, a verse from the Koran admonishing the believer to study nature in order to understand the mind of God. There was an American Indian in a blanket huddled close to an evening fire, the Hunger Moon glowing in the background to illuminate subtle patterns of wildlife among the naked trees all around him. There was even a deep blue cloth covered with elaborate patterns of silver snowflakes, for the atheists.

Betsy had these models on her walls, the patterns in stock, but it hadn't occurred to her to pull them together in a single display, until last night. She looked long at it, deeply satisfied. She had left two not obvious blank spaces in case customers came in with suggestions for other winter celebrations—and the name of a pattern she could order. There were growing populations of Hmong and Somali in the cities. Betsy wanted them to know they were welcome, too. Excelsior itself was mostly white Christian, but her shop drew customers from all over the area.

The sky was clear this morning, but the thermometer had fallen into the teens overnight. Any more precipitation between now and April would be snow. Betsy suddenly realized she was cold, and came back into her shop shivering and chaffing her arms. She went on through the back to start the coffee perking and the electric tea kettle heating. She'd had a cup of strong English tea with her breakfast bagel, but she'd need at least another to get her brain fired up.

She went behind the desk to put the start-up money in the cash register, check order slips and billing statements (the price of fuel oil was up again; thank God the new roof was deeply insulated). There was a note to remind her to phone Jimmy Jones, the man she'd hired last winter to plow the parking lot in back, to make sure he was on again for this winter; and another to say her accountant would be in on Friday to balance her books.

The door made its annoying *Bing!* (another note: replace that ugly noise!), and in came a tall woman in her late fifties, her full face marked with an emphatic pug nose. She had a lot of makeup on for this early in the morning. Betsy frowned—she was sure she didn't recognize her, but the woman looked familiar. Her brown hair was done in complicated curls and her gray winter coat had a beautiful silver fox collar. The woman glanced at Betsy, hesitated, then took a breath and approached the desk as if afraid she'd be sent away. Betsy hastily turned the frown into a smile of welcome.

"Good morning, may I help you find something?"

"I hope so," said the woman in a low, husky voice. "I'm thinking of taking up needlework. I did factory work all my life, and it ruined my hands." She held them out, and they were indeed work-thickened, though clean, and the nails carefully polished. "I'm retired now, and hoping to regain some fine motor skills by taking up a hobby. I first thought about music, but I was told I have no talent, so my brother recommended your shop."

"Oh!" said Betsy, recognition setting in. "You must be Mr. DeRosa's sister! You look a lot like him."

"Yes, everyone says that. We're twins, in fact. I'm Doris Valentine. Mick has said some nice things about you."

"Well, that was kind of him." Michael DeRosa lived alone in the smallest apartment upstairs and kept very much to himself. Betsy couldn't imagine what nice things he might have said about her; she couldn't have said anything at all about him, except that he always paid his rent on time. When the couple who rented the other apartment waylaid Betsy in the upstairs hall to complain about the smell of tar last month, he had stood shyly in his doorway, and only nodded in agreement when she looked at him.

"How long are you going to be visiting?" asked Betsy.

"Oh, just this week. But I've moved into the area, and will stop by often, I hope. Mick is my only surviving relative, and I want to spend as much time as I can with him." She looked around the shop and asked timidly, "Where do you suggest I start?"

"Have you ever done embroidery or knitting?"

"No, I'm afraid not. I can turn up a hem and sew buttons on, but that's all. My mother knitted, but she never taught me how. Not that I was very interested—I liked outdoor activities, horseback riding and softball."

Still ashamed of her frown, Betsy reached out with, "Me, too. In fact, I used to ride all the time. I keep making plans to take it up again, but never find the time."

"Did you ever try jumping?"

"Not in competition; to do that, you need a good horse, and we couldn't afford one. You?"

"I won a blue ribbon at our state fair the year I turned fifteen. But we had to sell the horse when Daddy lost his job, so that was the end of that."

"Too bad. Well, let me show you some of the things involved in stitchery. We also offer classes, if you don't live too far away to come in once a week."

"You know, I think I could manage that, if it turns out I have an aptitude for this stuff."

Betsy recommended Stoney Creek's wonderful and extremely basic *The ABC's of Cross-Stitch*, which Doris took, along with a book of simple patterns for beginners, a skein each of Anchor 403, 46, 305, and 266—black, red, yellow, and green—a roll of fourteen-count Vinyl-Weave, and an inexpensive pair of scissors. Betsy threw in a needle and a needle threader, told her about the Monday Bunch, and gave her a schedule of classes.

"Now, I tell you what," said Betsy. "Why don't you sit down in back for a while and try out some things from the book? Just shout if you get stuck, and I'll be glad to show you how to go on."

"Why . . . thank you," said Doris, a little overwhelmed at all this kindness. Betsy wondered where she'd gone to be told she had no musical talent. Funny how some shop owners seemed determined to put themselves out of business. Which of course just left more for those willing to go a little distance.

Betsy showed her how to use the needle threader, and then the door went *Bing!* and she went out to see who it was.

Godwin was taking off his gorgeous Versace leather trench coat to reveal a silk shirt in a heavenly shade of lilac under a purple vest. He said, "That window looks good, boss lady."

"Thanks for not complaining when I had my flash of inspiration and made you tear down the original."

"Aw, shucks, ma'am," he began in a teasing voice, then saw there was someone in back.

"Who's that?"

"Doris Valentine, my tenant Mr. DeRosa's twin sister. She's visiting for a week, and decided to try her hand at counted cross-stitch. Very much a beginner."

Godwin went back to introduce himself and soon had her trying out French knots and the satin stitch. When she'd finally had enough, she thanked them both profusely and departed, all smiles.

Godwin, amused by something, said, "Kind of fun to watch someone take those first steps down the road."

"Do you remember your first steps?"

"Depends on which road you mean." He waggled his eyebrows, grinned, and sashayed away.

"Give me strength," Betsy sighed and went to brew another cup of black tea. When she'd finished it, she called Alice Skoglund. "Would you care to have lunch with me?" she asked. "I want to talk with you."

"All right. Where? The Waterfront Café?"

"No, too many eavesdroppers. How about the sandwich shop right next door to me? He's featuring a tomato-basil soup that's very good."

"All right. Twelve-thirty okay? I'll meet you there."

8

There were two other shops in Betsy's building, a used-book store called Isbn's on her right and Sol's Delicatessen (though the owner's name was Jack Knutson) on her left. Betsy went into the deli. It looked as if it were original to the building and never redecorated, with a potted palm partly blocking the front window, large black and white tiles on the floor, and a long, white-enamel case faced with slanted panes of glass behind which were displayed cold cuts, cheeses, smoked salmon, salads, and a tray of enormous dill pickles. The stamped-tin ceiling was high.

The deli was mostly a carry-out place—there was a line of customers waiting to buy Sol's (or Jack's) wonderful thick sandwiches—but the owner had set up a couple of small, round, marble-topped tables and wire-backed chairs for the few who chose to eat in.

Betsy picked a chair that faced the door. She had barely sat down when the door opened and Alice came in. Tall for a woman in her sixties, and broad-shouldered, Alice wore a man's raincoat and sensible lace-up oxfords. Her eyeglasses had unstylish plastic rims.

Her face was set with grim determination, an expression that did not change when she saw Betsy and came to her table.

She sat down stiffly and said, "I know what you want to ask me. And I'm glad to tell you, get it off my chest. This is all my fault."

"What is?" asked Betsy.

But Alice's answer was forestalled by Jack's appearance at their table. He was a tall, bald man with tired eyes and a paunch that sagged into his white apron. His hands were covered with clear plastic gloves. "What can I get you ladies?" he asked, with a special nod to Betsy, his landlady.

"I'd like a mixed green salad with strips of smoked turkey on top, ranch dressing on the side," said Betsy. "Water to drink."

Alice consulted the menu handwritten on a white-board behind the white enamel case and said, "A cup of coffee, black, and a mixed meat sandwich with mayonnaise on an onion roll, please." Mixed meat meant ham, smoked turkey, thuringer, salami, and roast beef, sliced thin but piled high. Alice was not afraid of cholesterol.

When the man had walked away, Alice said to Betsy, in a low, shamed voice, "It's my fault Foster is suspected of murder."

"How can that be? You were saying he was innocent only yesterday."

Alice replied, "I mean it's my fault he's suspected, not my fault he did it—which I'm not convinced he did."

"I still don't understand."

Alice frowned and shifted around on her chair. "Maybe I should start at the beginning, which was when I realized Angela was afraid of her husband."

"What?"

"I said, when I realized Angela was afraid of her husband. Paul was a bully and a brute. And she wasn't timid, she was *intimidated*. I told her once that if she wanted to get away, she could come hide in my house. But she didn't even thank me, much less take me up on the offer."

"I don't understand. Why—how did you get involved?"

"My late husband was a pastor, you know that. Well, we both heard a lot of sad stories. After a while, you learn to look at people, and I could very plainly see that Angela lived in fear of her husband."

"If that was true, why didn't she leave him? After all, she had Foster to go to."

"True. But women stay in abusive relationships for a number of reasons. Fear of what he might do if she leaves is near the top of the list."

"So he really didn't love her."

"What he felt was nothing like love, it had nothing to do with wanting the best for the beloved, it had everything to do with control."

"How long were you aware of this situation?"

"I first saw it about eight or ten months before her murder. But Paul's smile had never fooled me, ever; more than once I saw him smiling when there was nothing funny or happy going on. But as I said, I saw

Angela looking unhappy when she thought no one was noticing. That worried me, and I offered to help her any way I could, but I wasn't the pastor's wife anymore, and anyway, I don't know how to be subtle, so I only scared her more. Then one Sunday I saw her talking to Foster after church. It seemed an innocent conversation, but friendly." Alice made a sudden curved gesture with a large hand, startling Betsy. She nodded. "Like that, Paul swooped in and just yanked her away. He was smiling, but for just a second there was a look on Angela's face that frightened me, she looked terrified. I phoned her at home that evening, pretending I wanted a recipe, and she seemed almost all right, you know what I mean?"

"Not exactly."

"I mean she wasn't crying, but she seemed anxious to get off the phone. Then all of a sudden I was talking to Paul, as if he'd snuck up and yanked the receiver out of her hand. I think he thought he'd caught her talking to a man, and when I said, 'Hello? Hello?' he said something like, 'Oh, it's you.' It was then I knew I had to do something."

"Why?" asked Betsy. "I mean, I understand completely how you could believe she was in danger, but why did you feel responsible for rescuing Angela?"

"Because I was the only one who thought she was in danger. I had talked to our pastor that Sunday, but he was a young man and—well, he was sure Paul was a good man and I was an interfering old woman. I couldn't call the police, they won't go over unless there's a loud fight going on that minute. And that organization that protects battered women won't take someone else's word there's a problem. There was no one else to tell; when people looked at Paul Schmitt, all they could see was that smile, all they noticed about him was how helpful he was to their neighbors."

"But you were sure he was a thoroughly evil man."

"Not thoroughly evil. He was like a lot of people, he put different parts of his life into different boxes. There was the Paul who programmed computers, the Paul who built cabinets for money under the table, the Paul who drove people home from the hospital. But I believe that at home there was a Paul who made his wife's life a living hell."

"Do you know why he did that? Not that she provoked him, nothing should provoke a man to behave like that, but what was it about him?"

"I don't know. Abusers happen for different reasons. In Paul's case, it may be because he needed to live up to that smile, he needed to make people think he was a good and happy man. And all the while, inside, he was afraid he wasn't good at all. Or that he wasn't good enough for Angela, who was a very sweet and gentle person—too sweet and gentle for her own good in this wicked world. Perhaps he was afraid someone would take her away from him. Do you know what I mean?"

Betsy nodded. "It's what used to be called an inferiority complex and today is called low self-esteem. Some people are sure that if people saw what they really are, they'd despise them."

Alice nodded back. "And he was sure Angela couldn't really love him, or that one day she'd meet someone truly good, and begin to see him for his real self. When my husband was pastor of our church, he dealt with abusive husbands surprisingly often. And even once an abusive wife, a dreadful person who terrorized her children and nearly killed her husband one night with a frying pan full of hot grease. I learned that you don't look only at someone's face, you look at the spouse's face as well. Paul was a smiler, but what I saw in Angela's face told me that she needed to leave him, or find someone to protect her from him."

"Did you ever see any bruises?" asked Betsy.

"Only once, the very next Sunday. She had finger marks around her wrist. She saw me looking and the shame in her eyes about broke my heart, but she hurried away when I tried to talk to her, and didn't come to church for two Sundays after that. So that's when I decided to put Foster in her way."

"Why Foster?"

"Because he seemed to be a good man, a nice man—and he had a way of paying attention to people. He was an usher back then, and he could spot a child about to get sick or a woman about to faint or a man starting to nod off, and get them away before they disrupted the service—and so they wouldn't embarrass themselves. And he was discreet, he never said a word to them or to anyone else afterward."

"Your church won't let people nap during the sermon?" asked Betsy, amused and diverted.

Alice smiled. "Oh, we don't mind the napping, it's the snoring that gets on people's nerves. Especially during the sermon."

Betsy laughed, then sobered. "All right, you knew Foster had an eye for trouble and a talent for averting it. He told me how you did it, by mentioning to him that Angela seemed unhappy. What did you think he would do?"

"The old-fashioned thing—throw a scare into Paul. Foster was taller than Paul, and he worked in construction, so he was strong. I wanted him to say something to Paul that would let him know we suspected he was cruel to Angela, and that he was prepared to take action if he wasn't nicer. That might have been enough, if I was right that Paul cared very much what people thought of him. But . . ." She sighed. "I had no idea Foster would fall in love with the girl. I feel very bad about that. And worse for what happened after." She lifted her head toward the ceiling and the lights blanked her glasses, hiding the pain in her eyes. "I wish with all my heart I never, ever said anything to Foster."

"So you think Paul murdered Angela."

Her head came down. She was surprised at the question. "Yes, I think that's most likely what happened. Abusive husbands, if they aren't stopped, go further and further until at last they go all the way to murder. I have heard he has an alibi, but Mike Malloy was the investigator, and I'm afraid Mike is not always good at his job."

"Did you tell Foster what you suspected?"

"No, of course not!"

"But you do think Foster murdered Paul?"

"I'm afraid that's possible. That beating Paul was

given before he was shot, that's the kind of thing an angry man would do. I can well understand that anger, I was angry myself when I heard Angela was dead." She was silent for a few seconds, then said bravely, because she was a good Christian and this went against her beliefs, "Betsy, if you find evidence that Foster killed Paul for murdering Angela, can I persuade you not to tell anyone? No matter how awful it is for Foster now, it would be far worse if he went to prison for murdering a man who badly needed to be killed."

Betsy said, as gently as she could, "I'm not sure it could be worse than what he's dealing with now. Nor am I convinced he did it."

Alice's homely face lit up. "Have you found something out?"

"No, nothing concrete. But don't you see? That's why I have to keep looking. If he didn't do it, the agony he's been going through for these past years is a gross injustice. And it's been hurting you as well, because you're blaming yourself for being an accessory. Just ask yourself: How would you feel if you found out for certain Foster was innocent?"

Alice blinked slowly, then nodded. "If you really could do that . . . Oh my, what a tremendous relief to have that burden lifted! Yes, then I hope you will continue your investigation. And may God guide you in your efforts."

Betsy went back to her shop to find no customers, and Godwin in an interesting mood, cheeks pink and his

movements somewhere between preening and strut-
ting, as if he'd won a fight.

"Guess who was here," he said as soon as she hung
up her coat.

"Who?"

"Foster Johns. Said he wanted to talk to you. But I
sent him packing." He snorted. "Don't look at me like
that! You've paid him for his services, and it's not as if
he was actually going to buy something!"

"Goddy, he needed to talk to me—and I needed to
talk to him!"

"Say, you don't believe that stuff Alice was putting
out, that he didn't murder anyone? No way, boss lady!
Why, I'm sure that when you get to the real facts of this
business, you'll prove once and for all that he did
murder Angela and Paul!"

"That may be true," retorted Betsy, "but I'm not setting out with that in mind! I don't investigate with an
eye to proving anything. I want to find out the truth.
But that means, Goddy, that I need to talk to Foster
Johns and anyone else I think can help. Which means
you don't run him, or anyone else you happen not to
like, out of the shop!" Betsy, her own cheeks flaming,
went to the back room to fix herself a cup of raspberry
tea. She sat down at the little table in the rear of the
shop to drink it and allow her blood to cool. She
shouldn't have snapped at him like that. Saying that
was over the line, and she was ashamed of herself. But
she wanted to talk to Foster and was annoyed Godwin
had prevented that.

And besides, Godwin had gone over his own line

more than once lately. It was part of his attraction in the shop to be catty. His "gay bitchy" riff was amusing, and customers liked it; it made them feel sophisticated to realize he didn't mean anything by it. And he had never been really cruel—though there had been a slightly unpleasant edge to his remarks lately. He was going through a bad patch—again—with his lover, she knew. That was enough to make anyone moody, but Godwin was in special circumstances.

She thought about that. Godwin had begun as John's "boy toy," and played the sweet young thing to John's mature protective instincts. The relationship had lasted far longer than was usual with these arrangements. John had seemed honestly in love with Godwin, and certainly Godwin loved him back. But Godwin's growing signs of maturity were stressing the relation-ship.

It was John's continued support of Godwin that enabled him to work for minimum wages and no ben-efits at Crewel World, so these signs of strain bothered her. Godwin had been around long enough to know better than to put off customers, and—her own stress notwithstanding—she had to find a way to remind him of that without reducing him to tears or making him angry enough to quit. Godwin at his best was a tremen-dous asset, and his knowledge of needlework was too important to her to risk losing him.

She heard the door signal go as someone came in, but Godwin, his voice only slightly too cheerful, took care of it.

She had nearly finished her tea when he came and

sat down across from her, a study in shame and gloom. "You don't like me anymore," he murmured.

"Of course I like you!" she replied at once, and was unhappy to note the edge in her own voice.

"Not really. You don't talk to me anymore."

"But I do, I talk to you all the time!"

"Not about important things. You didn't tell me you were thinking of hiring a general contractor instead of finding a roofer yourself, for example. I could have warned you about Foster if you'd said something. And you haven't been talking about Morrie. I have no idea how serious you two are. Are you perhaps thinking of selling the shop and moving to Florida with him?"

"No. He wants me to, but I'm not giving up this business. I enjoy the independence too much."

He smiled in bright relief, and she suddenly realized that here was another source of his distress. "Oh, Goddy, I should have said something, shouldn't I? Don't worry about your job here. This job is yours as long as I'm here, and I have no intention of leaving."

He smiled. "That's super! I'm relieved about that. Sad for Morrie, of course."

"Don't be. He can continue to use that house in Fort Myers as a winter getaway, I'm sure."

"Well, at least in the winter then you'll talk to me." His eyes turned serious. "That's what it is, right? You've got him to talk to, and that's why you don't talk to me anymore."

Betsy took a breath to deny that, found she was going to put it a trifle indignantly, and paused while she reconsidered her answer.

"See? I *knew* it! You tell *him* things you don't tell me!"

Betsy began to laugh. "Well, of course I do! I imagine you tell John things you don't tell me."

Godwin hesitated, then blushed deeply. "That's not quite fair," he remarked.

"Neither of us is fighting fair," agreed Betsy. "On the other hand, you have a point. I do confide in Morrie, and it's made me confide less in my friends, particularly you and Jill."

"Are you going to marry Morrie?"

"Not right now. That's a question for the future, the *distant* future." Godwin grinned in relief. "Anything else on your mind?"

"Do you really think Foster Johns is innocent?"

"It's possible."

"How *can* you think that?"

"Well, I talked with him. He *wants* me to investigate, Goddy. He's heard that I'm good at sleuthing, and he offered me money to look into his case. Would a guilty man do that?"

"Oh-kaaay," Godwin drawled, not willing to concede she had a point.

"Besides, Paul Schmitt really may have murdered Angela. He was very abusive to her."

"I don't believe it!"

Betsy told him what both Foster and Alice had said about Angela being afraid, and what Foster had said Angela told him about Paul's abuse.

"Strewth!" said Godwin, taking it all in. "That's incredible! Why didn't anyone else notice it?"

"Do you know, I think some may have. But Paul and Angela are dead and all anyone wants to remember is what a devoted couple they were."

"Yes, there is that tendency, isn't there? But think, suppose Paul murdered Angela. Doesn't that give Foster a super motive for murdering Paul?"

"Yes, it does. But he has an alibi for Paul's murder," said Betsy. "Confirmed by the police."

Godwin stared. "I didn't know that." Then he scoffed, "A half-assed one, I bet."

"Well . . ." conceded Betsy, and added, over his rising look of triumph, "But it was given to him by Paul Schmitt!"

That quashed him properly, but after she explained, he said, "Half the credit has to go to that cleaning woman—do you know who she is?"

"No, why? Do you?"

"No, but it would be interesting to know if she bought a car, or even a house, after the police let him go."

Betsy said, "Hmmmm. The thing to find out would be if he talked to her before the police did."

"Betsy, is it possible Paul was telling the truth, and he had evidence of who really murdered Angela? And then someone killed him to stop him showing it to anyone?"

"The police didn't find anything in his house. But then, if the killer came after him, he would have taken it away, wouldn't he?"

"Do you have any idea who this other suspect might be?"

"Not the remotest." But she was thinking of Vern Miller's warning to his son not to speak his brother's name.

9

Hello, Carol? It's Betsy at Crewel World. It's hard to know when to call someone who works at home, so if I'm taking you away from your work, just tell me when would be a better time to call."

"This is a good time, in fact; I'm rolling around the kitchen waiting for the water to boil for a cup of tea. What's up? More ghost stories?"

"No. I wanted to tell you that the new DMC colors are in, but also ask you if you'd be interested in stitching another model for the shop." Betsy sometimes asked experienced customers to stitch a pattern to hang on Crewel World's wall. A color photograph could not always do a cross-stitched pattern justice; it took an actual model to entice customers.

After some discussion, they came to terms for the stitching of Janlynn's complex Once Upon A Time, which was of a rearing unicorn about to be mounted by a medieval lady holding a spear with banners. "I'm sure it's lovely, but it sounds so incredibly Freudian, I'm surprised you dare to hang it in your shop!" said Carol with an amused gurgle.

The deal concluded, Betsy said, "You were saying the other day that your sister and Angela Schmitt were best friends. Is she a stitcher, by chance?"

"You want to talk to Gretchen about Angela, don't you?"

"Yes, I do. But I don't know her, and so I'm not sure how to approach her. I was hoping to do it through the shop."

"Well, she doesn't stitch." Carol paused in a pregnant way. "But she knits."

"Ah," said Betsy. "What level, beginner?"

"Just about. She's looking to try a sweater."

"Perhaps I should tell her that Rosemary is going to teach a sweater class in February. It's one of her most popular."

Carol made that gurgling sound that meant she was amused. "So not only are you going to pick her brain, you're going to pick her pocket. How much is the class?"

"Forty-five dollars, not including materials. Can she afford that?"

"From her change purse, probably. She married really well this time, and they go to New York City at least once a year to buy a bauble at Tiffany's and catch a Broadway show."

"Great. May I have her phone number? Or her e-mail address?"

Carol gave her both and they hung up.

Betsy was too busy to go upstairs and log on, so after she sold Mrs. Peters a winter solstice pattern and the floss she didn't already have to complete it, she picked the phone up again and dialed the number Carol had given her.

The voice that answered sounded so much like Carol's that for an instant Betsy thought she'd had a senior moment and dialed Carol's number again. But she glanced down at the number Carol had given her and her fingers recognized it, so she said, "This must be Carol's sister Gretchen. I'm Betsy Devonshire, of the needlework shop Crewel World."

"How do you do? Yes, I'm Gretchen Tallman. What can I do for you?"

Something in Gretchen's impatient voice made Betsy discard her roundabout ploy. She said directly, "I'm looking into Angela and Paul Schmitt's murders, and I'd like to talk to you."

"What do you mean, you're looking into their murders? Isn't Crewel World a stitchery store? Are you also a private investigator?"

"No, I'm working as an amateur. Foster Johns wants me to look into the case."

Now the voice was distinctly frosty. "Foster Johns? Isn't he the man who did it?"

"I'm looking for more information to see if I can figure out just who did it."

"But of course it was him!"

"He was never charged with the crime. Can you tell me something that can be used as evidence, so he can be arrested and brought to trial?"

"Wait a minute. If you're working for him, why would you tell the police anything I might tell you?"

"I'm not working for him, or for the police. What I'm looking for is some new evidence I can bring to the attention of the police."

"And they'll listen to you because . . . ?"

"Because I have discovered evidence in other cases. I have . . . connections in two police departments."

"Hey, do you know Jill Cross?"

"Yes, I do. Why?"

"What's your phone number there?" Betsy gave it to her, and Carol said, "I'll call you back," and hung up.

Ten minutes later the phone rang. Betsy picked up the receiver and said, "Crewel World, Betsy speaking, may I help you?"

"Okay, let's meet somewhere."

"Gretchen?"

"Who did you think?"

"Well, you sound a lot like Carol."

"So they tell me. Jill says you're all right, that I should trust you. So when and where can we meet?"

Betsy smiled, relieved Gretchen had called Jill and not Mike Malloy. "I'm working today, so you can come to the shop. Or we can meet for lunch, or after we close. We're open till five tonight."

"Lunch at Maynard's. One too late?"

"No. How will I know you?"

"They tell me I look like Carol, too. See you at one." Carol rang off.

Betsy was prompt, but a woman who looked a lot like Carol, except she wasn't in a wheelchair, was waiting, a highball in one hand. Maynard's was a waterfront restaurant, slightly upscale, with a large wooden dock running around two sides of the dining room. In the summer, the dock nearly doubled the seating area. This time of year it was bare of tables, and today the water beyond was gray and choppy. A wind-surfer made rooster tails across the bay, as sleek and anonymous as a seal in his black wet suit.

"You ever try that?" Gretchen asked Betsy as they sat down at their table, beside a big window.

"Not I," said Betsy. "I swim and I sail, but not at the same time. How about you?"

"Not for a while." Gretchen watched the surfer for a minute, giving Betsy a chance to study her. Gretchen could be either Carol's older or younger sister, it was hard to tell. There was a strong family resemblance, but she had that careless arrogance of a woman with a lot of money, which Carol lacked. Gretchen was lightly tanned and very fit, her blond hair streaked and cut in that expensive way that falls back into place with a shake of the head. Her hands were knobbier than Carol's, possibly because she was thinner, possibly because she was older. She wore pleated black trousers and a black cashmere sweater. Her Burberry was draped over the back of her chair. Her eyes came back to Betsy. They were large and a blue so dazzling that Betsy deduced tinted contacts.

"So why don't you think Foster Johns murdered a very dear friend of mine?" asked Gretchen.

"Because the same person who murdered her also murdered her husband, and Foster has an alibi for that crime."

"An ironclad one, no doubt. It's those watertight alibis that are so often carefully planned for, don't you think?"

"Sometimes," agreed Betsy. "But this isn't iron clad.

118

Paul called Foster and asked for a meeting. Paul said he had evidence of who really killed Angela, but that if he presented it to the police, they'd think he contrived it. But he said perhaps Foster would be believed. Foster agreed to meet Paul in his office on Water Street, but Paul never showed. Foster got out some paperwork while he waited, plans and figures, but he finally went home. His cleaning lady told the police the office was perfectly clean when she left, and Foster said he couldn't possibly have had time to both drive to Navarre to murder Paul and get his office that entangled in paper."

"If I were Foster, and I thought Paul murdered Angela because she was having an affair with me, I'd be damned if I'd agree to meet him alone. If Paul killed Angela for messing around with me, he might kill me, too. No way would I have agreed to meet him alone." She took a swallow of her drink and made a wry mouth. "Actually, I did meet him alone one time when I was me, and wouldn't do that again." She frowned. "I mean, I *am* me, and Paul's not meeting anyone again. But when he was alive I wouldn't have met him again at the Mall of America on the day after Thanksgiving surrounded by a platoon of cops on horseback." She made a big, sloppy circle in the air with her glass.

After a pause while Betsy made sense of that, she said, "How did you happen to meet him alone?"

"It was down at the docks. I'd been sailing with some friends and got in after dark. I'd had some vodka gimlets and was thoroughly shellacked. This was pretty soon after Angela said we shouldn't see each other anymore, so I never told her about it. Another thing I'm sorry about, because that might have been enough to pry her loose from that bastard. Anyhow, I came up the dock all by myself and I stopped by that kiosk thing on the shore, where they have announcements and historical information and like that inside it?"

Betsy nodded. She'd made a contribution to the Excelsior Chamber of Commerce and been rewarded with a paving stone outside the kiosk that came with the name of her shop cut into it. Most of the stones had names of individuals or companies on them; a few were still blank.

"The strap of my sandal was twisted so I was leaning against the wall of the kiosk trying to straighten it with a finger when all of a sudden he was there. I could see his teeth gleaming in the streetlight—he was always smiling, did I tell you that?" She blinked a little owlishly and Betsy wondered if the drink in her hand wasn't her third or even fourth.

"Yes, you did."

" 'Need a hand?' " he asked, all nice. 'Nope,' says I, 'I'm just fine.' And he kind of grabs me around the waist, only lower, and I slither away and say something like, 'How dare you?' only I put it stronger, and all of a sudden he's on me like paint on a fence, and I have this thing I do, where I stomp on an instep and it will make just about anyone alive yip like a dog and back off. Only all he says is, 'Hey, quit that,' and keeps on coming, so I send my elbow hard into his midriff, and he had to let go then, because he couldn't breathe anymore." She widened her eyes and shaped her mouth like a fish out of water, gulped a few times in imitation of a man with the wind knocked out of him, then chuckled maliciously. "That was the only time I ever saw him without that damn grin." She lifted her glass and drained the liquid, tonguing the ice to shake loose the last of it.

"Good for you," said Betsy as Gretchen put the glass down with a victorious thump. "Nice to be able to take care of yourself like that."

"Well," said Gretchen, tossing her head to make her hair shift and fall back, "when you start moving in the upper class, you either learn or go under." She snickered.

"When you heard about Angela, did you think right away that Foster Johns murdered her?"

"Of course not. I was sure Paul did it." She stared out the window, those amazing eyes filled with tears. "He pretended to be a nice person, but he didn't have many friends, though lots of people are saying now how much they liked him. I went to high school with Paul, and even back then I thought there was something wrong with him. It was like a glass wall between him and you. He was always smiling and doing favors, but you couldn't get close to him. And it didn't change after he married Angela. He was nice to me, but all he'd talk about was sports or fishing or hunting—never about anything deep or important. I sometimes wondered if he didn't have any deep thoughts. There was just this weirdly happy guy, with a smile a yard wide—and an inch deep."

"How long had you known Angela?"

"Since middle school. She was like the opposite of Paul. She was really shy, but when you got to know her, she was deep. I remember when she was twelve, she had worked out what it must be like after you died. She said time was a river and we rode down the river all our lives, seeing the shoreline in sequence; and then when we died, we were like flying over the river and could see where it started and all the places it went and where it ended. And everything that ever happened or was going to happen was all happening on the river, so that's why God knew what we were going to do before we did it. I mean, she was *twelve,* and she had this all worked out. I was the only person she told. She was good with books and tests, but her grades suffered because she almost never talked in class. There were some boys she liked in high school, but she never went out with them because she was too shy to let them know she liked them. I was the wild and crazy one, dances and parties and midnight movies, and people used to ask me why I liked Awkward Angie, and I'd say, 'But she's so *deep!*'" Gretchen laughed self-deprecatingly.

"So why did she marry Paul?" asked Betsy.

"I asked her that once and she said, 'Because he asked me.' I think she had a real self-esteem problem, she could have done *so* much better if she knew what a great person she was."

Their waitperson brought the big menus at this point and there was a pause while choices were made. Gretchen ordered another Manhattan, Betsy a sparkling water; Gretchen ordered a big salad, no dressing; Betsy a salmon steak that came with fresh fruit and a frozen yogurt dessert for fewer than a thousand calories.

"What did Angela tell you about Paul?" asked Betsy when the menus were taken away.

"That he was wonderful, outgoing, and always cheerful, with lots of friends. That was at first. Then she said less and less and finally didn't say anything. Then it got hard to get hold of her, and she finally said Paul didn't like her to spend so much time out with her friends, he wanted her at home with him. Well, I was working on wrecking my first marriage about then, so what the hey, we didn't move in the same circles anymore and it was easy to let things slide." Gretchen shrugged, but her mouth was weighted down by regret. She rattled the ice in her empty glass, looked around and brightened. "Here come our drinks, about time."

When their entrees arrived, Betsy said, "If Paul was such a nasty piece of work, he must have had enemies. Any idea who they might be?"

"Not a clue. Angela never said anything about him having trouble with anyone, and I don't remember anyone else saying they hated his guts. You really believe Foster Johns didn't whack him, don't you?"

"I don't know anything for sure right now. I do believe the only way to prove whether or not he did it is to find out who had a motive to kill both of them."

"Well, don't look at me. After that encounter at the docks, I could have cheerfully shot him, but there's no way on earth I would have killed Angela." Her voice broke. "Oh, Angie, my sweet angel!" She snatched up her napkin and held it to her nose and mouth. "I hope you find out who it was, with proof and everything. I want to hire the worst lawyer on earth to defend him."

Back in the shop, Godwin said, "I hear you're moving up in the world, lunching at Maynard's with Gretchen Goldberg-Tallman?" He walked in a circle, nose in the air, arm lifted and bent at the wrist. "How *do* you do?"

"The FBI and CIA should come and study the grapevine in this town," declared Betsy. "They could throw away their wiretaps and bitty cameras and position-locating satellites. The frozen yogurt hasn't even melted in my stomach, and you have a full report. Is Gretchen all that high in society?"

"Ooooh, first-name basis and *everything!*" said Godwin.

"Goddy . . ."

The young man knew that tone, and sobered. "Yes, she moves in the upper circles, dinner with the Daytons, weekends with the Humphreys and the Wellstones. Len Tallman's name turns up on the lists of Minnesota's most wealthy—plus his father's grandmother was Teddy Roosevelt's granddaughter. Gretchen's a trophy wife, his third; he's her second husband."

"Carol didn't strike me as someone who moves in those kinds of circles."

"She doesn't. Len says Carol makes him uncomfortable, so Gretchen doesn't see much of her sister."

"Len dislikes Carol because she's a lesbian?"

"No, because she's in a wheelchair. He has a 'thing' about handicapped people. He'll give a million to charity or a research hospital, but he can't bring himself to touch a person with any kind of handicap."

"How do you know this?"

"Well, rich people need lawyers, and who is my beloved John but one of the best? John is also something of a gossip."

"Has John ever said anything about Foster?"

"Only that he must be pretty slick to get away with murder. Foster's not a client; John gossips mostly about his clients."

Betsy's eyes narrowed. "I wonder what would happen if Len Tallman were ever injured so severely he'd need special aids to get along."

"Can't happen," said Godwin. "He's got living wills on file around the world, saying let him go if it's worse than a bad chest cold. I heard he's even got DNR tattooed on his chest. Oh, by the way, the *Bay Times* called. Number's on your desk."

The *Excelsior Bay Times* was a weekly newspaper given away free but widely read. Expecting to be connected with somebody trying to persuade her to buy a bigger ad, Betsy dialed the number and found herself talking to a reporter.

Someone had told him about Betsy's "Winter Window," and he thought it would make a nice little article. He proposed to stop by with a photographer at Betsy's convenience. About an hour later, she was posed beside her window, smiling broadly, and the reporter took at face value her comment that she liked diversity and hoped her window would bring a diverse collection of customers to her business.

That evening, Betsy had Foster Johns to dinner. It was supposed to be Morrie's dinner, but by the time she'd gotten hold of Foster, it was too late to have him come back to the shop. So she'd called Morrie to explain that she needed to talk to Foster, and Morrie had been fine with that.

Foster arrived at her apartment looking tired. He seemed to have lost ten pounds—and also that controlled air she had noted about him. "How are you doing?" she asked, taking his jacket. He was wearing Dockers and an old gray sweatshirt.

"Could be better, could be worse. I lost a client in Chanhassen today; apparently some idiot here in Excelsior phoned him. If I find out who did that, I'll sue his ass. Maybe some of the gossips in this town lose their house for slandering me, they'll think twice before they spread lies. But on the other hand, two women in the Excello Bakery smiled at me yesterday. One of them was Alice Skoglund, but I don't know who the other one was."

"Alice is definitely on your side, she's hoping I'll find proof of your innocence," said Betsy. "Wine?" He nodded, and she filled his glass. "She's been feeling guilty because she wanted you to threaten Paul Schmitt with a poke in the nose if he wasn't nicer to his wife, and instead you ended up falling in love with her and then suspected of her murder. Here, come and sit down; the chicken will take a few minutes more to bake."

Once he was comfortable, she asked, "Why did you agree to meet Paul the night he was murdered?" she asked.

"Because I wanted to know who really murdered Angela," Foster replied.

"You believed he had the evidence?"

"I didn't know what he had. He said he had something, and he said the police might not believe it if it came from him."

"Weren't you afraid to meet him alone?"

"Hell, yes! But this was three days after Angela's murder, and the police hadn't arrested anyone. I was going crazy. I was sure as I could be that Paul did it, but when he called, he sounded so sincere, it kind of threw me. But I'm no fool, I also figured maybe he was thinking to round things off by killing me, too. But I thought, well, what if he really has something? So I told him to come to my office. I set up the recorder in the top drawer of my desk, and I left the drawer open about an inch. I walked around the office saying 'Testing, testing,' and adjusting the volume so it would pick up his voice no matter where he was. And a lot of good it did me. I'm sure I bored some unfortunate cop out of his mind when he had to sit and write down everything he heard on that recorder, which was me saying 'Testing, testing' about twenty times, then fragments of me wadding up paper, scratching lines and figures on paper, swearing, and whistling through my teeth. But because it only came on when it heard a noise, it didn't help much with the alibi because it didn't record the long periods of silence."

"And you didn't phone someone to tell him you were meeting Paul, in case they found your body the next day?"

"No. It was supposed to be a secret, him turning the evidence over to me. If he really had something, then I was more than willing to be his cat's paw in getting it to the police."

"Do you remember who your cleaning lady was back then, the one who helped give you an alibi?"

He smiled. "Sure. She's the same one I have right now. Her name's Mrs. Nelson. Treeny Nelson. You want to talk to her?"

"Well, yes, I think I do."

He said, "Call me tomorrow and I'll give you her phone number. Or come by at five and wait for her."

10

The next day Betsy was busy unpacking and putting out items from Dale of Norway's Trunk Show. The boxes came from Needlework Unlimited in Edina. Betsy was pleased to see that not only was everything there, it had been carefully packed. Dale of Norway sold beautiful sweaters at Hoigaard's and The Nordic Shop and at upscale stores at the Mall of America. But they also sold patterns and wool. Betsy mooned over the authentic Norwegian sweaters that served as models—she put one pattern aside for herself, a typical snowflake-on-sky blue one—but there were also some lively and beautiful nontraditional patterns. She was particularly taken by a dark gray scarf with pockets at either end, whose orange edging was finished with little picots. It was worked with two strands of wool, making it thick and heavy, but also quick to work. Perhaps Jill would like it for Christmas, if it were worked in shades of blue. (Betsy sometimes thought Jill became a police officer because she could wear blue to work every day with nobody thinking anything of it.) She put one of those patterns aside as well.

She removed the small paper sign announcing the show from her glass-fronted door and replaced it with a much bigger one, which also offered fifteen percent off all knitting materials. The trunk show would be here for a week and then move on to Duluth.

She had no more than hung the new poster up when three women marched into the shop, one an adolescent twelve, the next old enough to be her mother, and the third old enough to be her grandmother. Betsy didn't recognize any of them as regular customers. The girl had dark brown eyes and the dark auburn hair that sometimes accompanies them. She said, "I need a kippah for my bat mitzvah, and they"—she tossed her head in the direction of the other two women—"didn't like any of the ones for sale at Brochin's." Which was a store in St. Louis Park.

In a heavy Russian accent the grandmother said, "What did she say? What's a kippah? We are here for a yarmulke. I want to stitch a yarmulke for my granddaughter. Bad enough they do this bat mitzvah for girls, but if they do, I want something nice in blue and white. You have such a thing?" She looked around doubtfully.

The girl said, "Kippah is the correct term for it, I learned that in Talmud-Torah school."

The mother said, "It doesn't matter." And to Betsy, "My mother-in-law said she would sew one if you had a yarmulke pattern or even just a circular pattern we liked in the right size." She made a round shape about six inches across with her thumbs and fingers. Her English came from Brooklyn with just a trace of Russia in it.

The daughter said firmly, "I want something pretty, with horses on it. Or soccer."

The grandmother said something in angry Russian, the mother replied in kind, and the daughter shouted, "Speak English!"

"You hush!" said her mother. "Your grandmother wants to make you a gift, and so what if she calls it a yarmulke and you call it a kippah? It comes to the same thing, so why do you always want to make trouble?" She turned to Betsy, and, her voice suddenly sweet, she asked, "So, what do you have?"

Betsy had spent some years in New York City, and this was so much a taste of there, she could not stop smiling.

"I have some needlepoint yarmulkes, but only a few. Let me show them to you." She pulled four canvases from a drawer in the white dresser near the front door, and the child immediately picked a pink one with black

130

silhouettes of dancing children around its edge.

But the grandmother wanted the blue one with white Stars of David. The child refused to even consider putting such a lame article on her head, which scandalized her grandmother no end. "What are they teaching you at shul, how to be rude?" she demanded.

Another shouting match began, into which Godwin walked, his arms full of boxes picked up from the post office. He was so startled at the racket that he dropped them, which in turn startled them into silence.

"What's going on?" he asked.

"A little disagreement over what pattern of yarmulke the young woman is going to wear for her bat mitzvah," said Betsy.

The fight started in again and faintly, in the background, Betsy heard the phone ringing. At this point she'd had enough of New York and withdrew gratefully to answer it, taking the cordless phone into the back of the shop.

It was Alice. "Is today the start of the trunk show?" she asked in her deep voice. On being assured that it was, she asked Betsy to not sell the last of any mitten patterns until she had a chance to come by "probably tomorrow" and take a look at them.

Betsy promised and then said, "You seem to have disliked Paul Schmitt for a long time. Surely you weren't the only person who didn't like him. Alice, I'm trying to find someone who hated him, perhaps someone he hurt badly. Can you think of anyone like that?"

Betsy had to wait while Alice sank into her noisy

131

coma for a minute, thinking. The sound cut off. "Alex Miller, maybe," she said.

"Jory's brother?"

"That's him."

"Why?"

"Because Alex and Jory were supposed to go into partnership with their father in that auto repair shop Vern founded. Then there was a family fight that kept getting worse and now Alex isn't speaking to either his father or his brother, nor they to him. His mother told me that Alex blames Paul, but even now, with Paul dead all these years, the quarrel hasn't been made up. Alex's wife, Danielle, talked to Alex's mother about it, but she can't get them to make peace. Alex is the one most hurt, he was really close to his brother and wanted to go into business with him so his father could retire, but that's not possible anymore. Jory can't do it all alone, so Vern has to keep working. Vern's wife is worried about him. She and I work on several committees together and we talk."

Betsy recalled the angry way Vern Miller and his son Jory had talked about Alex. "What does Alex do?"

"He works at the Ford plant in St. Paul."

"Do you know where he lives?"

"No, you'll have to ask Mrs. Miller. Vern won't speak to Alex, but I'm pretty sure Jin stays in touch, for the sake of the grandchildren."

Betsy hung up, then realized the quarrel out in front had stopped. She went out for a look and found Godwin alone in the shop. "What happened?" she asked.

132

"I sold them that round needlepoint canvas with the ocean theme. The grandmother is going to stitch the ocean in a solid blue and the fish in very pale shades of gray and white, so she gets her Israeli flag colors and the daughter gets sharks, dolphins, and a beluga on her yarmulke."

Betsy heartily approved of this clever solution. "I wish you'd been here instead of me when they came in," she said and immediately changed her mind. "No, it was fun to hear the accents again. Do they have a Jewish neighborhood in the cities?"

"There's a suburb called St. Louis Park that has so many, they call it St. Jewish Park."

Betsy was startled. "I didn't think there was anti-Semitism in Minnesota!"

"Why not? We're just like everyone else. There's even a small KKK chapter. Every time they parade, the onlookers argue over whether the Klansmen are stupider than they are ugly or uglier than they are stupid. But St. Jewish Park isn't a slur, the nickname was given by the Jews who live there."

"Oh," said Betsy, and went to call Vern Miller's wife.

Jin Miller spoke unaccented English, but in a soft and gentle voice without the flat tones common in middle America. "Why do you want to talk to Alex?" she asked.

"I'm hoping he can tell me something about Paul Schmitt."

There was a little silence. "He will not say anything good about that man," Jin said.

"That's all right, I'm not looking for only good things."

"You are the woman who investigates murders, am I right?"

"Yes."

"And you are looking for the name of the person who murdered Paul and Angela?" Jin asked.

"Yes."

"I can tell you that. It was Foster Johns. He was in love with Angela, and when she told him she would stay with her husband, he killed both of them. The police didn't have enough proof to arrest Mr. Johns."

"Perhaps I can find the proof, one way or the other."

"Oh, I see." A little pause. "All right, if you think Alex can help, I will give you his number."

At a little before five, Betsy left Godwin in charge and hurried the few blocks up to Foster Johns's little office building. His receptionist said Foster had already left on a consultation, but that Betsy was welcome to wait; she wanted to speak to their cleaning lady, right?

"Thank you," said Betsy, and sat down in the little reception area to look at a copy of *Architectural Digest*. She was studying an ad featuring a sumptuous easy chair, when the door opened and a short, stout woman with a snub nose and blond hair well mixed with gray came in. She wore a puffy winter jacket of sky blue with big yellow patches, and heavy mittens, which she pulled off after closing the door. She greeted the receptionist in a quiet, dour voice, then saw her nod toward Betsy and turned to look.

"How do you do," said Betsy. "Are you Mrs. Nelson?"

"Yah, that's me. What can I do for you? I warn you right now, I'm not taking on any new customers."

"No, this isn't about that, I just have some questions for you, if you don't mind."

Mrs. Nelson looked at the receptionist, who said, "Mr. Johns said she'd be by. It's all right. Why don't you use his office?"

"Yah, okay," said Mrs. Nelson. "It's back this way."

She went around the big desk that stood in front of a paneled oak door, Betsy following. It opened into a room with tilted tables and big windows and, when Mrs. Nelson threw the switch, merciless fluorescent lighting. To the right was another paneled door, and this led into a very comfortable office with a modern leather couch, an antique desk, and a big, plain table. One wall was made of corkboard. A single blueprint was tacked to it; otherwise the table and desk were empty. There were framed architectural drawings on the other walls.

Mrs. Nelson went to the couch but didn't sit down. "What did you want to ask me?"

"Do you remember the night Paul Schmitt was killed?"

"Do I? Ha! You bet I do! The police come and get me out of bed in the middle of the night—no, *past* the middle of the night, it was like three A.M.! Want to know if I cleaned Mr. Johns's office. Of course I cleaned it. I give it a once-over every night and a heavy cleaning once a week, more often if it needs it. They said did I clean it that night and I say sure, and they ask me what did it look like when I got there. They couldn't wait till a decent hour of the morning? I asked them."

"You understand how important it was to get the answer to their questions, don't you?" asked Betsy.

"Yah, sure I did, but only later. What they wanted was to know if Mr. Johns murdered Mr. Schmitt. They didn't tell me that then, so I was cross with them, like anyone would be, waked out of a sound sleep."

"So what did you tell them?"

"That the big workroom was kinda messy, but the office was neat, only the wastebaskets was full. So they took me back to look, and what a mess! Paper and blueprints and drawings and all, everywhere."

Betsy asked, "Had you ever seen it like that before?"

"Yah, sure. Whenever he's workin' on something, he hasta get everything out and he sticks some of it up on the wall with thumbtacks and lays other stuff on the table and his desk, sometimes on the couch even."

As if reminded, she unzipped her jacket and sat down. "And he leaves it out, spreads it around, rearranges it, whatever, until he knows how the project's gonna go, then he cleans it up."

"He never asks you to put it away?"

"Oh, no, no, I know better than to touch any of that there stuff. I dust and I vacuum and I empty wastebaskets and I scrub the toilet and every once in a while I do the windows."

"What's he like to work for?"

"Well, I used to hardly ever see him, y'know. That

was good, because when he would stay after special, it was so he could complain about something. He was a real shouter, and he went through receptionists like they was Kleenex. I'm surprised I stuck with him, and maybe I wouldn't've, but the place is easy to clean, no grease or mud. Then after this murder thing he calmed down a lot. He used to give me a Christmas bonus, but now I get another one, on my birthday."

"Mrs. Nelson, do you think he murdered those people?"

She looked at Betsy, surprised. "Yah, I do. Everyone knows he did it. I think it made him sad and that's why he's nicer than he was. It was almost good for him, in an awful way. He's suffered and he's still suffering, worse maybe than bein' put in jail. I hope they never prove he did it." She looked at her hands, small but red and thickened. "Surprised me, it did, coming into that office and seein' all that paper out, because when I left it, there wasn't so much as one sheet of paper showing."

"But you don't think that proves he was here at work rather than over in Navarre shooting Mr. Schmitt?"

"No, I don't. It'd take maybe ten minutes to pull out papers and drape 'em all over everything, wouldn't it? Didn't prove a thing to me."

Betsy thanked her and went back to the shop to find Godwin selling her tenant's twin, Doris Valentine, a set of Christmas tree ornament patterns and floss.

"Hi, Betsy," she said in her husky voice. "Godwin says, can I make an ornament to put on the tree." She beamed at Godwin. "*Such* a nice young man!"

137

Godwin said, "I wouldn't usually ask someone so new to cross-stitch to commit to doing that, but Doris is an unusually hard worker, and she's doing really well."

Doris simpered a bit. "Well, I have such a good teacher. He was just showing me how to grid." She held up a scrap of evenweave fabric basted in rows five threads apart.

Betsy smiled at both of them. "I remember how great it was when someone showed me about gridding. All of a sudden counted cross-stitch became actually possible for me. I'm glad Godwin has taken the time to show you; he's a good teacher. This isn't a difficult craft to master, but it helps to have someone show you the steps to take."

11

Alex Miller worked second shift over at Ford Motor Company, where he was a line supervisor. He was suspicious and reluctant, but at last said that if Betsy wanted to talk to him, he'd meet her at the gate to the plant at 11:00 P.M. tonight, when he was on break.

Betsy called Morrie and he agreed to drive her over after she closed, and watch from the car while she talked to Alex.

She spent the next several hours, between customers, going over her stock, straightening, sorting, removing anything worn or frazzled, putting things back where they belonged. Keeping up with tasks like this made inventory less of a chore.

When she first inherited Crewel World, she'd often found a pattern or painted canvas tucked out of sight under or behind other items—a flower canvas pushed in among the Christmas ones, for example. At first she attributed it to absentmindedness, or the stress of trying to learn how to run a small business with a large and varied inventory. But now, settled in and comfortable with the work, it was still happening. A Laura Doyle Sea Images cross-stitch kit was hanging near the back of the Marc Saastad flower kits. "Look at this, Goddy," she said, exasperated. "Am I getting senile? Already?"

"What's the matter?" asked Godwin, and came for a look. "No, it's not you," he said, amused. "When customers want something and don't have the money at hand, or when a sale is coming up, they'll hide what they want so they're sure it will still be there when the sale starts. I've done that at Macy's, put a sweater I want in among the extra-extra large sizes, so it will be there when I come back with my credit card."

Betsy began to laugh, her relief so great that she forgot to be annoyed at her sneaky customers.

But between trying to restore order and serve customers, who were turning out in great numbers now that office hours were over, there was little time to worry, or even sit down. Betsy was beyond tired when she finally turned the needlepoint sign around to "Closed." She made three mistakes on the deposit slip and had to do it over twice before it was right. She sent

Godwin yawning off with the money and slip, turned the lights off, punched the code for the alarm system, and went out the front door, yanking it shut and pushing it hard to make sure it locked.

Morrie was already waiting outside, engine running. She clambered into his Jeep Wagoneer for the forty-minute ride, and fell asleep before they were halfway to Minneapolis.

Morrie began to shake her gently as they crossed the short bridge into St. Paul at Minnehaha Falls Park. "Hello? Hey, sugar, wake up!"

"What?" said Betsy sleepily. She looked out the window as he pulled to the curb beside a very large, single-story brick building across a wide sidewalk. A familiar logo said "Ford." "Oh, are we there already?" She thrust her fingers into her hair and pulled hard to wake herself up. "Why'd you let me fall asleep? Now I'm all groggy!"

"What do you mean, 'let' you fall asleep? I talked to you, I played the radio, I whistled—loud and badly— to the music, and you fell asleep anyway. Maybe we should call this off for now and try again later."

"No, no, it was hard enough to get him to meet me the first time. What time is it?"

"Ten fifty-eight."

"No time to go scrounge up a Coke then. Well, here's luck." Betsy climbed wearily out of the Wagoneer. The rain had stopped, but the temperature had dropped, and the icy wind whipped her coat around her legs and tousled her hair as she walked up to the high chain-link fence that surrounded the plant. A stocky man in a dark leather jacket and wool cap was just coming to a halt by the truck-size gate.

As Betsy got closer, she could see that he looked very like his brother. "Alex Miller?" she said, closing the distance, and he nodded. "I'm glad you agreed to see me."

"What's this all about?" he demanded gruffly.

"Paul Schmitt," she said.

"That son of a bitch? I suppose you're another one of those who wants to canonize him!" He turned to walk away.

"I think you may be right to hate him!" she called, and he turned around, one eyebrow lifted in surprise. "I'm here to find out the truth!" she declared.

"If I told you the truth about him, your ears would burn for a month!" he declared.

"I used to be in the Navy, where I dated a bosun's mate. I doubt if you could surprise me."

He came back to grab hold of the fence with all his fingers and describe in ugly, graphic terms what he thought of Paul Schmitt's mind, heart, and organs of generation, the various perversions he practiced on victims of many species, and the likely entertainment his soul was giving the devil at present.

"Mr. Miller," Betsy interrupted firmly when he paused to regroup his imagination, "this is all very interesting, but you gave me only ten minutes, and I have some questions to ask."

He snorted, then relaxed and put his hands back in his pockets. "All right, ask away."

"Do you consider Paul Schmitt somehow responsible for the breach between you and your brother Jory and your father?"

Alex's eyebrows rose high on his forehead, then came down again. "Well, how did you figure . . . ? Yes, I do. He played all three of us, one against the other, until now neither Dad nor Jory will speak to me."

"Why would he do something like that?"

"For the fun of it, I guess."

"Why would he think it was fun to do that?"

"Because he was a low-down, filthy, sneaky, grinning snake, who—"

"Seriously," said Betsy, cutting him off before he could get all wound up again.

Alex rubbed his jaw, then his face, then the back of his neck. "My wife got onto me the same way you are," he said. "Saying there had to be a reason. And what we finally came up with is, because he saw me kiss his wife on the cheek. Before God, that's all I can figure."

"When did you kiss his wife on the cheek?"

"About the time her mother died. I went to the funeral and when we were shaking hands after, I leaned over and kissed her. She was looking sad, and just shaking her hand didn't seem like enough. But she kind of jumped back like I did something wrong, and looked around kind of nervous, and there was ol' Paul, looking at me like a lightbulb had gone on over his head."

"Did you know he was a very jealous husband?" asked Betsy.

"Oh, yeah, he was always suspecting her of playing

142

him for a fool. But we were friends, Paul and me, or I thought we were, and he didn't say anything to me about it, so I thought she explained it to him, and he was all right with it. But right about then I started having trouble with Dad and Jory. I never connected Paul to that, they never mentioned him, so it never occurred to me. And then Danielle, that's my wife, started acting suspicious toward me, accusing me of playing around. It was getting to the point we were talking divorce when Paul was shot dead—and damned if things didn't start coming around right again with Danielle. I was just grateful that things were straightening out, again I never thought about Paul. But Danielle noticed it, too, and she sat me down and made me talk about it. I told her I didn't know why things were better, I wasn't doing anything different. But she said that wasn't so, that before I'd been acting like the biggest jerk in the world, and now I wasn't. And I repeated I wasn't doing anything different now than I was before. And after she quit shouting at me about how I'd been fooling around on her—which I wasn't, and where did she get that idea, and why was she trying to have a baby behind my back, and we fought over that for a while, and then she said stop shouting and listen to me. And we figured it out. I didn't even know she'd been talking to Paul, and all along it was Paul's doing. At first I couldn't believe it, and then I did, and it was like the sun coming up. And after a couple of days I started thinking of the fights with my brother and Dad. I wanted to ask them about it, but they wouldn't talk to me, so Danielle went to Mom, and the two of them figured it was the same thing between me and Jory and Dad, pretty much. Only it's too late to do anything about that, I guess."

He heaved a big sigh, lifted his arms in an exaggerated shrug, then pointed a thick forefinger at Betsy. "You can't imagine how grateful I am to Foster Johns for shooting that bastard. It was too late for Jory and Dad, but at least he saved my marriage for me."

"I don't understand," said Betsy, wondering if she was so tired she was missing something obvious. "How did Paul Schmitt work it so you quarreled with people?"

"Well, suppose someone your husband thinks of as a good friend tells your husband he better start using a condom because you want another baby and you've quit taking your little daily pill? And then this 'friend' comes to you acting all concerned and says he thinks you ought to know that he and your husband went to this whorehouse together and your husband now has a social disease. So you think your husband's using a condom because he's got the clap, and your husband thinks he better use one if he doesn't want another mouth to feed, which he can't afford. And this 'friend' tells your husband to tell you that he's using condoms because he heard that the brand of birth control pills you're using isn't always effective, and then he tells you that he heard your husband say the lie he's gonna tell you is that he's using condoms because he heard there's a bad batch of birth control pills out there."

Betsy, trying to keep track of who she was supposed

144

to be and fuddled by all the pronouns, said, "You mean this was happening to you? I'm not sure I understand what Paul was up to with all this running back and forth."

"He was causing serious trouble between Danielle and me. I mean, pretty soon I was ruining my back trying to sleep on the couch and Danielle was dropping ninety-pound hints about rent-a-slut, which I didn't understand. And the kids were looking like refugees from a war zone, which it just about was at our house. I will never, ever forget the day my wife made me sit down for a talk and there it came to us, we figured the whole thing out. It wasn't me, it wasn't her, it was Paul, him carrying lies back and forth to the both of us. That was the biggest relief I ever felt, it was like I'd been drowning and got saved at the last minute. I actually thought I was going crazy there for a while, my whole life was coming apart and I couldn't figure out why. And all the while it's this bastard who's pretending to be my friend—and all I can figure for a reason is because he saw me kiss his wife!"

"You also think he played that same kind of game to ruin the relationship with your brother and father?"

"I don't think, I know it. Jory and me was tight like Siamese twins all our life, but Paul played him and my dad first, just like he played me and Danielle later. He convinced me Jory wanted Dad's business all for himself, and told Jory I wanted him out, and told Dad we both wanted to give him the shove. I never even heard of someone doing what he did, not in real life. While it was happening it was like a combination *Twilight Zone* and one of those spy novels where everything's a double cross." He held his watch up to catch the light and said, "I can't talk anymore, I got to get back to the line."

"Thank you, Mr. Miller," she said, but it was to his back, because he'd already turned to walk away.

Betsy was shivering with more than cold on her way back to the Wagoneer.

"What'd he say?" asked Morrie as she climbed in.

"He's either totally paranoid or Paul Schmitt was a dreadful, cunning person." She repeated Alex's story.

"What do you think?" asked Morrie.

"He's sure he's telling the truth. And I'm halfway to believing him. I've already gathered that Paul was a jealous, suspicious man, always prepared to believe someone was making a play for Angela. And back in junior high he had a talent for getting other people in trouble."

Morrie asked, "Did you ask Alex where he was the night Paul was killed?"

"No, why?"

"You *are* tired, Kukla. If Alex figured this out while Paul Schmitt was still alive, he had one hell of a motive."

"But he said he didn't start figuring it out until things started to straighten out on their own."

"And that may even be true."

Betsy rode in a thoughtful silence all the way home.

It was nearly midnight before they got back, which meant a second night Betsy did not get enough sleep;

146

and this time not even the thought that Morrie had to be at work an hour before she did comforted her.

The story of her window would not appear in the newspaper for another week, but word apparently was spreading anyway, because the next morning there were two customers Betsy had not seen before waiting at the door. They wanted the dreidel canvases.

Four more followed soon after, one wanting a knitted Christmas stocking pattern, the bright-colored wool, the bobbins, and a pair of knitting needles. She said she hadn't knitted in years, but the window had inspired her to knit one for her grandson. The others were regulars, but they, too, remarked that the window was exciting to see, and one signed up for Rosemary's January knitting class.

Jill, currently working nights, came in yawning, saying she was shopping before going to bed. She bought some Kreinik gold cord and stayed to look at a new shipment of hand-painted canvases. She lingered over an M. Shirley canvas, a big tree in winter with small birds or animals on every branch. It was complex, beautiful—and four hundred dollars. Phil, a retired railroad engineer, came in to pick up a kit he'd ordered, and sat down at the library table to open it and make sure all the colors were there in the right quantity. He soon had that dreamy look all fiber fondlers get as he sorted, smoothed, and straightened the flosses, knotting them onto a floss stick, plotting his angle of attack on the pattern. Jill sat down to talk with him.

Two more women came in to buy the snowflake pattern, and another wanted the Hunger Moon pattern. Betsy was making a note to order more copies of both when the door made its annoying *Bing!* sound. Betsy looked around to see who was coming in, and didn't even notice the little silence that fell, because she was herself immediately focused on the tall, handsome stranger standing right inside the door. He was somewhere in his thirties, dressed in a fleece-lined leather jacket that was either old or expensively "distressed," a white turtleneck sweater, and Dockers pants. His hair was dark, falling casually over a broad forehead. His eyes were dark, too, with early signs of laugh lines around them. His firm jaw was marked with a trace of beard shadow. His mouth was wide with a hint of sensuality, his shoulders filled the jacket, and his stomach hinted at sixpack perfection under the sweater.

In Los Angeles or New York, he'd be an actor or a model trying to become an actor. Here in Excelsior, Minnesota, he had to be someone's husband.

Betsy looked around to see which of her female customers was looking at him possessively. Everyone, of course. Even Godwin. Especially Godwin, who was the first to move, heading toward him, lips eagerly parted. But the man brushed past him to stop at the desk and say, "I'm looking for a counted cross-stitch pattern of a dog, just the head, preferably." His voice was slightly rough-edged, perfectly designed to tickle in private places. "I saw in the Spring preview of *The Stitchery* magazine that Stephanie Hedgepath does any breed to order, but I accidentally threw my copy away, and don't know how to contact her."

Betsy almost said, "Huh?" just to get him to talk some more, but got a grip and said, "I keep the more popular patterns in stock, including Hedgepath's. Which breed are you looking for?"

He smiled, happy to reply, "A golden." Because about every third purebred in America is a golden lab.

"I'm sure we have several patterns you could use."

She went into the back to help him sort through the rack of cross-stitch animal patterns. His hands were broad with slightly knobby fingers, and without a wedding band. *He can't be married,* thought Betsy; *no wife would let a husband who looks like this wander around with a naked third finger.* Several of her customers decided they were interested in animal patterns, too, and came to look. Interestingly, one of them was Jill, whose only usual foray into counted was small Christmas tree ornaments.

Godwin hovered, making helpful noises. Even Sophie, the fat shop cat, came to rub gently around the man's calves—but perhaps she thought there was a sandwich in his pocket.

The man selected a pattern of the head of a golden lab, a piece of green evenweave to do it on, a set of stretcher bars, and a needle threader—"I'm into rotation, so I keep a threader on each project." The only sign he gave he was aware of the stir he was causing was the wink he gave her as he paid for his purchases. He strode to the front door and was gone.

"Strewth!" exclaimed Godwin, one hand splayed across his chest. "Who was *that?*"

"I never saw him before," said Betsy.

"He paid with a check," said Jill. "Read his name off it, will you?"

"Oh, he's got to be Elmo Slurp or something equally awful," said Godwin. "There has to be *something* imperfect about him."

"I don't think so," said Betsy, putting it in her cash drawer and shutting it firmly. "The imperfection here is that each of us has a perfectly nice boyfriend."

"Oh, yeah," sighed Godwin. And Jill gave a little nod, as if waking from a pleasant dream.

"I'm available," announced Phil, who had gone to the window to watch him drive off. "Not that I'm gay, but did the rest of you notice he drove off in a Porsche? Hell, *I* might consider converting for a rich man who does counted cross-stitch."

Laughter broke the mood satisfactorily. But Betsy said, "Goddy, can you come back and show me that trick with the coffee urn?"

There was no trick with the coffee urn, it was what Betsy said when she wanted to talk to Godwin out of range of eavesdroppers.

"Sure," said Godwin, following her back.

Betsy shut the door. "Are you all right?" she asked.

Surprised, he replied, "Yes, I'm fine." He felt his forehead worriedly. "Why, do I look sick?"

"No, not sick, but your reaction to that handsome customer made me wonder just how bad things are between you and John. You've told me before he gets upset if he thinks you're flirting with someone else. If this is how you behave around good-looking men, maybe John is right to feel threatened."

"Oh for heaven's sake, there's no rule that says a man can't *look!* Anyway, there's nothing seriously wrong between John and me right now. Well, nothing newly serious. Not *that* serious."

"Goddy . . ." Betsy was pulled between compassion and annoyance.

"There's nothing you can do about it. There's nothing *I* can do about it, either. He's so cruel and suspicious right now, he *drives* me to behaving badly! He'll get over it, he always does. It's just that when he's like this, I get to thinking what it might be like with someone else. Someone like—"

"Mr. Lightfoot?"

"Is that his name? Too *dreamy!* What's his first name? Where's he from?"

"His first name is Rik, spelled *R-i-k,* and he's not from Minnesota." This wasn't exactly true. His check had been printed with a Montana address, but lines had been drawn through it and a Minneapolis one handwritten beside it. His bank was a national chain with local branch offices.

"Where, then? Iowa? Wisconsin?" Betsy put on her best poker face. "Oh, not farther? Where, then? I don't remember an accent. Don't tell me he's from Atlanta!"

"I'm not going to tell you, or anyone else."

"*Wait* a minute." Godwin's blue eyes narrowed. "I thought you didn't take out-of-state checks."

"Perhaps in his case, I made an exception." But her cheeks burned, and Godwin grinned.

"He *is* local, isn't he? Well, well, well, I wonder who's in line to have his heart broken, John, Lars—or

Morrie?" He fluttered out.

Betsy followed more slowly, thinking. How deep was her affection for Morrie when a pretty face—all right, a truly gorgeous face, not to mention body—could turn her head like that?

The shop remained busy until a little after one, when it abruptly became empty. Betsy had had a cup of coffee and a slice of untoasted raisin bread for breakfast and her stomach began making nonnegotiable demands for lunch. She said to Godwin, "I'm going to run down to the Waterfront Café for a sandwich, then to the pet shop to get some cat food. Can I bring you a sandwich or something?"

Godwin said, "If the café has a nice-looking apple, buy me one, otherwise I'll take three ounces of bunny kibble." He pinched at his waist. "I'm up two pounds and the holiday season is on the horizon." He flexed his upper right arm, squeezing it tenderly with his fingers. "I'd better rejoin my health club, too. This pretty boy doesn't want to get all flabby."

Godwin, barely but still in his twenties, was engaged in a struggle to stay seventeen, which meant slim but not skinny, athletic but not muscular.

Betsy went out into the chill and walked briskly down Lake to Water Street, then up half a block to the small café on the other side of the movie house. She went in and was greeted by name by the young woman behind the counter and two late-lunch customers. Two women sitting in a booth raised their hands in a tentative wave. Betsy sat in the single booth under the front window.

152

The Waterfront Café's feature that day was their hearty but not very spicy chili. Betsy had a big bowl further thickened with crackers—she was a cracker crumbler from way back—and a small milk.

She had only taken a few bites, when someone sat down across from her. She looked up and saw a slender man with light blue eyes and a thin mouth set in a face dusted all over with freckles: Detective Sergeant Mike Malloy.

"Well, well, Sergeant Malloy," she said. "What brings you in here?"

"You do. I went to your place and Mr. DuLac said you were here." He leaned forward. "What's this I hear about you?" he asked in a low voice—the Waterfront Café was Gossip Central in Excelsior, and he was obviously unhappy being seen even talking to her. Two customers sitting at the counter had swiveled their seats around to look.

Betsy replied equally softly, "What have you heard about me?"

"That you're poking around in the old Schmitt double murder."

"Do you object to that?"

Surprisingly, he grinned. "If you can prove once and for all who it was who killed Angela Schmitt and her husband, I'll be the happiest cop in the state."

"So it's all right with you if I continue to look into things?"

He sighed. "I'm not empowered to stop you. But I do want to warn you, this involves someone who has murdered twice. Someone who apparently still has the gun he used on Angela and then on Paul. You haven't got the training or the experience to deal with the kind of person who would do something like that."

"Thank you for being concerned—no, I really mean that. I know you think I'm a silly, interfering amateur, and in a way you're right. There are times I wonder what on earth makes me think I can do this. But it keeps happening, and I keep getting it right. If I do find things out, or have questions, may I come to you?"

He made a face and seemed about to say no, but changed his mind. After all, she had solved a couple of baffling cases. "What kind of questions?"

"Did you think at first, when Angela was shot, that Paul had done it?"

He shrugged. "You always look at the husband. He seemed nice enough, and he'd never been arrested for anything, but I never liked that smirk of his."

"What about his alibi?"

"Aw, it was okay, but I would've liked it better if someone had come into the gift store and seen him. There were some other oddities, too, but not enough to make an arrest. Then someone beat the crap out of him and then shot him with the same weapon . . ." He tugged a freckled ear. "That put paid to any idea he did it. Except . . ." He held out one hand, palm down, and waggled it slightly.

"What?" asked Betsy.

"If you weren't a damn civilian . . ." He said, and stopped yet again.

She decided not to argue with him. After all, she *was* just a damn civilian, with no badge or private eye

license. She straightened in her seat and took a delib-
erate bite of her chili. It reminded her of her mother's
chili; it even had elbow macaroni in it. She took a sip
of milk, then dipped her spoon into the chili again.

"All right, all right," he grumbled as if she had been
arguing with him. "There were powder burns on his
trousers where he was shot, on his head, and on his
hands. This means the gun went off very close up. This
tends to mean self-inflicted wounds."

"But the beating wasn't self-inflicted, surely."

Malloy nodded. "I know. I thought maybe someone
came and beat him up for killing his wife, and Schmitt
shot himself after that person left, maybe with an eye
to framing whoever beat him up. But who? And then
where's the weapon? It's gone. It's never been found."

Betsy leaned forward to ask quietly, "Is it possible
he could have thrown it out the door or out a window
before he died?"

Malloy shook his head. "With a bullet in his brain?
Not a chance. He was dead before he hit the floor." He
shrugged. "Anyway we went over the whole property
with a fine-tooth comb. The only possible conclusion
is that someone shot him, and took the gun away with
him."

"The same gun that shot Angela."

"Very probably. We never recovered the slug that
killed her. It went out the window and, for all I know,
fell into the back of a passing pickup and was carried
away."

Betsy smiled incredulously. "Is that possible?"

He shrugged. "All I know for sure is, six of us

looking damn hard couldn't find it. But we recovered the shell casings and they're all the same caliber and the mark of the firing pin on all of them is identical." He glanced around the café, but the men on the stools had turned away again.

"How conclusive is that?"

"Pretty good. Not as good as the marks the rifling of the gun barrel would've left on the slug, but pretty indicative."

Betsy took another bite of chili. "So what did you decide about the gunpowder burns?"

"That it was close-in fighting. A struggle for the gun."

"Did Paul Schmitt own a gun?"

"Yeah." He looked uncomfortable, and added, "See what I mean? This whole case has screwy parts to it. The gun was registered, and it's the same kind of gun that was used in the murders. And it's gone, too."

"Did Paul Schmitt report it missing before the murders?"

"No. He told us he had a gun when we first talked to him, but when we went to his house for a look at it, he couldn't find it. He said he had no idea how long it had been missing. I thought he'd tossed it away after using it on his wife, and I wanted to arrest him right then, but there just wasn't enough evidence."

She asked, "How sure are you that Foster Johns did it?"

For the first time, Malloy spoke in full voice. "Damn sure! He was on the scene of Angela's murder at the time it happened. We've got three or four witnesses to that. He has a half-assed alibi for Paul's murder, but I think he could have rigged that. I hauled him in and grilled him good, but he wouldn't break. So I had to let him go. I wish he'd leave town—just seeing him walking around free grates me hard."

There was a little murmur that ran around the café, and one of the men sitting at the counter grinned at the other.

Malloy left, Betsy hastily finished her chili and went to the checkout counter. There was a bowl of apples and pears sitting by the cash register, so she chose the biggest apple and paid for it with her bill. As she stuffed it into a pocket, she looked around the little café, and there in a back booth she saw Foster Johns looking like a man waiting to be hanged.

12

Betsy went out into the chill air and up the street, past the beauty parlor and the bookstore. She paused a minute to look in the pet shop window. A lop-eared rabbit nosed about its low, wide cage, and two white kittens with blue eyes and just a hint of darkening on their ears and tails were tangled into a shifting, complex ball in their big cage. One was trying to chew the ear off the other. A bearded lizard in an adjacent aquarium was watching them with a beady eye.

She went in. The shop was warm, the air moist and redolent of small animals and pet foods. Canary and parakeet noises filled the air. The aisles were crowded with items—it was a small shop, but tried to meet the needs of a large variety of pet owners. Betsy went down the aisle that catered to cat owners, then to the front counter, where a curly-headed blond was allowing a man in a raincoat to hold a friendly parrot on the edge of his hand. The bird was gray with a red tail.

". . . two thousand," the shop owner was explaining.

"Does that include the cage?"

"No, a good cage will run you another thousand. Plus you'll want some toys. African greys get bored easily, and they have a poor response to boredom."

"Hmmm," said the man.

"I looove you," crooned the parrot in the blond's voice, and bent its head, asking to be tickled on the neck. The man complied and the bird made a low chuckling sound of pleasure.

"He's nearly two and already has a vocabulary of about a dozen words," said the shop owner. "We call him Gray Goose, but you can change that."

Betsy, thinking of Godwin being unhappy in front of customers back in her shop, and Foster being desperately sad in the café, said impatiently, "I can't find the Iams Less Active."

"It should be right beside the Science Diet Hairball."

"The Science Diet is there, but no Iams."

"I'll clip those for you if you like," said the shop owner to the man, who was now lifting the compliant bird's wing. She went back for a look and agreed there was no Iams Less Active on the shelf. "I've got some down the basement, can you wait a minute?"

"Sure," said Betsy. She went back to watch the man ask the parrot to step from hand to hand as if on a Stairmaster, which it did obediently.

But when four minutes had passed and the woman hadn't come back, Betsy went to the open basement door for a look. The steps were thick old wooden boards. There was only silence coming from down there.

Cautiously, Betsy started down. There were shelves and stacks of crates forming crooked aisles on the floor. The lighting was of the harsh fluorescent kind, but too widely spaced, so the place was full of sharp shadows.

Betsy heard a rustling and dragging sound from halfway down a dark aisle and started toward it. Then she stopped and stared. "Hey!" she said.

"What?" said the shop owner, turning around. She had two seven-pound bags of dry cat food in her hands.

"The basement of this place is *huge!*" Betsy could see through the backless shelf the pet food had come off of. There was a wall made of rough old boards, but the boards were badly warped, and the ceiling light shone through them into a big space beyond. And judging by where the basement stairs were, the board corresponded to the wall of the pet shop above.

"Oh, sure," said the shop owner. "My store is the middle of three in the Tonka Building."

"Tonka Building?" Like most people, Betsy went around gawking upwards at buildings only on vacation. The buildings on this block formed a single solid row, and the entrances to each store were different in design, so she hadn't realized three were in a single building. Betsy's own building had three shops in it, but the building had open space on either side, making the arrangement obvious. Here, the Tonka Building was up against the next building, which was a beauty shop, which was next to the Waterfront Café. Were the beauty shop and café in a single building? Betsy had no idea.

This was for a moment merely interesting.

But if the pet shop was the *middle* of three, why, "Then Heritage II on the corner, your Noah's Ark, and Excelsior Bay books next door are all in the Tonka Building."

"Sure. And a CPA, a dentist, and a chiropractor have offices on the second floor."

"Are you saying it's possible to go from one of the three stores to another without going out in the rain?"

"Not through the shops themselves."

"Not now . . ." agreed Betsy, pausing hopefully.

"Not ever, there never were any doors," said the shop owner, handing Betsy a bag of cat food and picking up a third. She headed for the stairs. "Of course, there used to be gates between the board walls down here, but they were nailed shut years and years ago."

"Gates? There are *gates?* Are these walls original? Were there always gates in them? How long ago were they nailed shut, do you know?"

The woman stopped on the third step and turned to look at Betsy, surprised at her interest. Then she looked

160

around the basement, thinking. "Well, it was divided like this when I started Noah's Ark, and that was nine years ago. I'm pretty sure the walls between the basements went up shortly after the auto dealership moved out of the corner store, and that happened in the early sixties, I think. The building itself dates to the forties."

"But when were the gates nailed shut?"

"They wouldn't open when I moved in, so longer ago than nine years."

"Oh." Betsy looked back along the shelves. They were sets of shelves rather than one long shelf, but were put right up against one another. They were made of dark gray metal with X bracing at the ends. They ran the parallel to the walls and formed two aisles. They were sturdy, which was good, because the one against the wall was crowded with bags and cans of pet food. That would, however, complicate the life of someone trying to come through from the gift shop. He would not only have to pry out the nails in the gate, he'd have to unload a shelf and crawl across it, then put it all back together again on his way back.

"Hold on a second, okay?" said Betsy. She went quickly to the other side of the basement and found the situation even worse for a potential crawler-through; the shelves were laden with heavy and frangible glass aquariums and goldfish bowls, big boxes of filtering kits and lights, and weighty bags of gravel.

"Come on, Betsy, if Goose hasn't bitten Mr. Winters, I think I've got a book-balancing sale waiting for me."

"All right," sighed Betsy.

But upstairs, watching Mr. Winters write out a very

large check while his new friend chewed the buttons off the epaulets of his raincoat, she had another idea and said, "Excuse me, Nancy, but may I ask you something?"

"Certainly, in a minute. That's right, Mr. Winters, with tax that comes to two thousand, two hundred thirty-six dollars and fifty cents."

"Those shelves down in your basement. They're very nice. Where did you get them?"

"At Ace Hardware, right across the street."

Betsy nodded. Ace Hardware's building had suffered a fire and the store had pulled out of the building two years ago, but people talked about the hardware store as if it were still there.

Nancy continued, "I'm sure they're a standard item, so if you want to drive over to Highway Seven and 101, you'll probably find them at the Ace there. They're nice, because they're strong, easy to set up, and on sale. I can't remember how much they were, not that remembering would help, I've had them for about three years. Before that I only had a single row of wooden shelves down the middle of the room."

"Really?" said Betsy, and Nancy looked up from writing the sales slip, surprised that Betsy was pleased. "Listen, would you mind terribly if I went down for another look? Thanks, Nancy!"

Before Nancy could object, Betsy went back down the stairs. Over on the side with the aquariums—"Why didn't she put these in the middle?" grumped Betsy— she began very carefully lifting items off the shelf where the gate was. The shelves blocked access to the gate, but Betsy leaned into the shelf opening where the gate's handle would be. There were about two inches of space between the gate and the back of the shelf. Betsy grasped the handle—a thick wooden C that didn't operate a latch—and pulled gently. The gate didn't give. She pulled harder. Still no give. The reason why was right there, too; she could see the slotted backs of rusty metal screws that held the edge of the gate against its frame. Just like Nancy had said: nailed shut. Well, screwed shut.

Betsy backed out and carefully put things back where she'd found them.

She went back upstairs, where Nancy was explaining to a new customer that the black-and-yellow canaries were a wild variety whose song was prettier and more varied than the domesticated solid yellow.

She waved at Nancy as she went by, put seven dollars and change on the counter for the cat food, and hurried out. She went next door, to the bookstore.

"Hi, Ellie-Ann, I'm in a hurry, but I need you to do me a really large favor."

"Certainly, if I can."

"Let me go down in your basement and poke around a bit. I'll try not to move anything, and if I do, I'll put it back."

Ellie-Ann looked doubtful, but Betsy said, "It's about Angela Schmitt's murder."

"Oh, my God, really? Then go ahead, go ahead. Here, let me show you where the light switch is."

The entrance to the basement was through the far

end of a storage closet behind the checkout counter, which was near the center of the north wall of the store. The stairs were concrete, and the basement was clean but cluttered, like a storage place not open to the public tends to get. There was a wooden plank table with a microwave and small office refrigerator on it, and in boxes all around were surprisingly few books, some bright book posters, a supply of stuffed animals and puppets (a feature of the Excelsior Bay Bookstore), props for their display window—Betsy recognized four slender, white-barked birch trees from last spring—and the teapots and coffee urns brought out for author appearances.

There was a clear space along the boards that divided the bookstore's basement from the pet shop's. Betsy found the gate to the pet shop near one end of the clear space. It didn't open to a push from this side, either, though there were no screws in evidence here. She looked across the pet shop space—Betsy had neglected to turn the lights off—and wondered if, in the gate on the opposite wall, there were screws on the gift shop side or the pet store side.

A voice behind her said, "What are you looking for?"

Betsy jumped and came down facing Ellie-Ann. "Mercy, you scared me!"

"Sorry. Is that what you were looking for? Yes, it's a door; no, you can't open it, it's been nailed shut since before I took over the store; yes, there's another one on the other side of the pet shop; no, it hasn't been tampered with, either." Ellie-Ann was obviously repeating replies to questions she'd been asked before. She smiled and explained, "Mike Malloy looked at it after Angela was killed upstairs."

"Ellie-Ann, what did you think of the investigation? Were they really thorough? Could they have missed something?"

"I'm no judge, of course. But actually, they did miss something. They had to come back and do a better search before they found it."

"Was it something to do with the gate?"

"How could it be something about the gate? It's there, it doesn't open. No, it was a shell casing. When Mike didn't find one the first time, he said the gun was a revolver. But they found shell casings at Paul's house after he was shot, so they came back and they searched some more, and they found one."

"That's interesting."

"Is it? It made me wonder if they didn't miss something else. I was pretty sure Paul shot Angela, y'see. That is, until I saw in the paper that Paul was murdered; and with the same gun, which they couldn't find. So I guess it wasn't another of those dreadful murder-suicide things."

"Did you know Angela was having an affair?"

"No. I suspected she and Foster Johns were attracted to each other. He developed an interest in books he hadn't shown before Angela started to work here, and she always seemed especially pleased to see him. But I had no idea it was a real affair. I don't know how they managed it. Paul kept such careful track of her, it was ridiculous." She added, almost irrelevantly, "Paul did some good things in that gift shop, but he was rude to browsers. Once he insulted a man dressed in dirty jeans, who turned out to be the mayor's brother, visiting from Arizona, and a very wealthy man. He'd been helping Odell paint his boat when he suddenly remembered it was his wife's birthday." She chuckled. "He came in here instead and bought a copy of every book about Minnesota I had in stock and asked if there was a jewelry store and a flower shop in town, and left at a fast trot."

Betsy tugged at the wooden handle of the gate, which still refused to move. "Why were there gates here in the first place?"

"I don't know," said Ellie-Ann. "Maybe in case of fire?" She shrugged. "The man I bought the bookstore from said the doors were nailed shut when he moved in, and that was eleven years before I took over, and that was six years ago. So it's at least seventeen years since you could go from one basement to the next."

Discouraged, Betsy went upstairs to retrieve her bag of Iams Less Active. As she went out the door, Ellie-Ann called, "Betsy?"

"Yes?"

"Please, solve this one, will you? Angela was a sweet person, and she didn't deserve to die."

13

The next morning Betsy, feeling much fresher after a good night's sleep, came down to find another new customer waiting in the doorway. She was an elderly woman in a long, dark blue coat, a red knit hat pulled down over her ears. She huddled close to the door because, while the sun was shining painfully bright, there was a cutting wind blowing and the temperature was in the mid-twenties.

Betsy hastily unlocked the door and let her in. "Good morning," she said. "Come on, sit down. If you can be patient a few minutes, I'll finish getting open for business. There will be hot coffee or tea soon, too."

"Thank you," said the woman, easing herself gratefully into a chair at the library table and pulling off her red mittens. Sophie jumped up onto "her" chair, the one with a powder-blue cushion, and looked the customer up and down briefly before deciding this was not a Person With Goodies. The cat settled down for a nap.

Betsy busied herself with lights and cash register, then went into the back, and soon the warm smell of coffee brewing wafted into the shop.

"Now," said Betsy, coming back to the library table, "what can I do for you?"

The woman said, "My name is Florence Huddleston, and I am a retired school teacher. Alice Skoglund said

I should come and talk to you, because Paul Schmitt was a student in my seventh-grade English class many years ago."

Betsy pulled out the chair next to Ms. Huddleston, turning it so it angled toward the woman, and sat. "What can you tell me about Paul?"

"Nothing as an adult. But I remember him quite well as a seventh grader. He was a bright boy but an average to poor student, because he was lazy. I once told him he should grow up to run a charm school, because he could be very charming when it suited him, and he was forgiven too often. But his real talent was in laying the blame for his misdeeds onto others, and for getting others to behave badly while maintaining his own— what is the modern word? Deniability. I'm certain these traits continued into adulthood, as many do. Certainly they seemed innate in Paul. And another thing: He wasn't really brave, of course; people like him never are. But he had a curious ability to ignore pain that made him seem brave. He once broke his left wrist in a lunchtime wrestling match, but on his way to the nurse's office he stopped in my classroom to say why he wasn't coming back this afternoon. He pulled that horrible arm out of the front of his shirt and displayed it like a trophy to the two girls I was tutoring. There was no doubt it was broken, it was swollen and the fingers were purple. But he so enjoyed shocking and frightening me and the girls, he couldn't resist the opportunity."

"He doesn't sound like a very charming boy to me, if he could do things like that."

"Surprisingly, even I sometimes found him charming. He was very popular among many of the students and even some teachers. He was generally helpful, taking half of a load, opening doors, picking up after people, and he was always smiling and polite. That charm was as real as his deviousness. But I remember he used to fascinate a certain set of boys and even some girls with a gruesome collection of true crime stories."

Betsy, blushing faintly because of her own helpless fascination with crime, sat back to absorb this for a moment, then asked, "You didn't by chance know Angela Schmitt—well, she wasn't a Schmitt back then—the girl who married Paul?"

"Angela Larson. I know she was in my class, but I can't remember her at all. She came into the classroom on time, did her homework, scored well on tests, but never volunteered anything in class. Teachers love students like her, the invisible ones, because they make the larger classrooms bearable. I only know about her because I looked her name up in my class records after she was murdered. According to my diary, she was a B-plus student who wrote a rather good paper on *The Mill on the Floss*."

"How about Foster Johns? Was he also a student of yours?"

"Yes, he was." The old woman touched her mouth with slender fingers, picking her words carefully. "He was a very bright young man, but aggressive, impatient, and hotheaded, a dangerous combination. He was a very competent artist, but he wasted that talent drawing cartoons of, er, scantily-clad women with extraordinary physical endowments. He was funny and popular, but with that streak of wildness, I often wondered how he would turn out. I was pleased to learn he'd tamed his creative talent by going into architecture, but sadly disappointed to discover his impetuous affair with a married woman, and worse, that his temper led him to murder both his mistress and her husband."

"So you think Foster Johns murdered Paul Schmitt?"

"Yes, of course, and Angela as well. Isn't that what you have set out to do, prove it once and for all?"

"I'm trying to discover the truth, and I'm not convinced Mr. Johns is guilty."

"Whom else do you suspect?"

"Well, did you have the Miller brothers, Jory and Alex, in your class?"

"Not Jory. He heard I was very demanding about grammar and he signed up with Mrs. Jurgens, who allowed vernacular and even ungrammatical language and phonetic spelling. Alex was forced to take my English class because Mrs. Jurgens's class conflicted with a shop class he wanted."

"What an extraordinary memory you have!" Betsy said.

Ms. Huddleston laughed gently. "I do have a good memory, but most of what I'm telling you came from the diaries I spoke of. I went back through the years pertinent to your investigation before coming to talk with you."

"I'm pleased you kept them, then," said Betsy.

"Oh, they are often useful to me. Whenever I hear about a person's success, it is a special joy to me to look in my diaries and find I not only gave him high marks in my class, I predicted his future success. And when someone does something shocking, I will look to see if I predicted that, as well. I'm not always right, but more often than mere chance would have it. I think character is formed early."

"So what did you write about Alex Miller?"

"That he was not nearly as interested in the mechanics of good writing as he was in auto mechanics. That he was touchingly loyal to his friends and family, and would probably go into some kind of partnership with his brother when he came to adult-hood."

"Yes, too bad about that," said Betsy.

"Well, as I said, these predictions of mine don't always come true."

"It nearly did; he wanted to join Jory with his father in his auto service company, but someone instigated a quarrel between him and them."

"Do you know who the instigator was?"

"Alex says it was Paul Schmitt."

"But Paul and Alex were close friends when they were my students! I remember that because I thought no good would come of it."

"And that's probably what happened. There was a breach when they were in their twenties, and Alex now blames Paul for setting his brother against him, and causing his plans to go into the family business to fall apart. The quarrel was very serious."

"So you think it's Alex rather than Foster who might have murdered Paul?"

"He was still murderously angry at Paul when I spoke to him two days ago, and Paul has been dead for five years."

"Oh, dear. That's so dreadful. Do you think it possible that Paul was in fact responsible for the breach?"

"I'm afraid I do."

"Oh, my. Oh, if you are right, that is truly dreadful." She stared at the surface of the library table. "I knew Paul was a troubled child, and I was afraid he'd have an unhappy life. But I didn't know it was to be so short. It was bad enough to think that two flawed youngsters such as Foster and Paul crossed paths to the deadly injury of one of them, but to think that Paul is responsible for an essentially decent fellow to go so terribly wrong, that is indeed a tragedy."

She stood. "I had intended to buy a kit of Christmas ornaments from you," she said. "But I no longer have the heart to work on them. I'm sorry."

"I'm sorry, too," said Betsy. "Perhaps at a later date. Christmas is still nearly two months off. Meanwhile, won't you have a cup of coffee or tea before you go? It's so cold outside."

"No, thank you. I think I'll just go on home now."

Betsy watched her going up the street seemingly unaware of both the cheerful sunlight and the cold wind that whipped around her.

Godwin had the day off and the part-timer scheduled to come in had the flu, so Betsy had to work alone that day. Her customers seemed more impatient than usual, and more inclined to take things off the racks or shelves and put them down anywhere (even into their pockets and purses). They didn't like her herbal tea, the coffee was too weak (never mind that it was free), and why didn't she have the Mirabilia pattern the customer had driven all the way from Anoka to buy?

The talk with retired teacher Ms. Huddleston colored her morning. On the one hand, it saddened her, because it reminded her the people she was investigating had once been children full of promise, who were hotheaded and impetuous, malicious and manipulative, loyal and unscholarly, rambunctious and impatient. Character forms early, Mrs. Huddleston had said. So on the other hand, trying to see the hopeful child that still lived behind the eyes of her demanding customers helped Betsy stay friendly.

Toward noon she went into the back to get down a new package of foam cups from a high shelf—only special customers got the fancy porcelain ones—when the step stool wobbled and she grabbed at a lower shelf to steady herself. The shelf, which held the aforesaid porcelain cups, as well as containers of imitation and real sugar, cans of coffee and tea, stir sticks, and creamer, broke loose. Down came Betsy, the shelf, and its contents—and the three-gallon coffee maker, which was half full of very hot coffee.

Betsy yelled in fright and pain, and the tiny back room was immediately jammed with all five customers present, who got in one another's way and shouted contradictory orders at her and one another.

Betsy managed to get her feet under her and with a faint cry of, "Hot! Hot! Water!" pushed through the little mob into the rest room where, sobbing, she turned on the cold water and tried to cool her burning arm.

Once that was taken care of, she looked down at her red knit dress, bought new barely a week ago. Coffee and wet grounds had made huge dark patches all over it. Unless it went into cold water immediately, it was ruined. She'd have to go upstairs and change.

But how, with a shop full of customers?

Wait a minute, hadn't one of the customers been Bershada? Bershada, the retired librarian, who therefore knew how to deal with the public.

She opened the door a few inches to peer out, looking for a dark face wearing glasses. And found it.

"Bershada, could you do me a big favor?"

"I hope so," said Bershada. "What is it?"

"I have to go change clothes. Could you possibly watch the shop for just five minutes? You don't have to collect any money, just answer questions until I come back down. And maybe keep anyone from leaving with merchandise they haven't paid for yet."

"Sure, I can do that."

Betsy slipped out the back door and down a short corridor to another door that let into the entrance hall of the apartment stairs. She hurried up.

Her keys were in her pocket, and in two minutes she was in her bedroom, stripped to her underwear. Which also had to be changed. She put her dress into the bathtub and turned on the cold water while she went to get dressed.

174

But there was no time to rinse out her hair, which was damp on the back and right side. "There must be no coffee on the floor down there, I think I soaked it *all* up!" muttered Betsy.

Four minutes later, resplendent in jeans, chambray shirt, and head scarf, she went through the back door into her shop.

Where she was met with applause and laughter.

"Well, I know I've got a heavy clean-up job ahead of me," she announced. "I might as well dress for it."

The rest of the day was as if every customer present at her accident went home and phoned her friends, who all decided they had to come and laugh at Betsy looking awful and stinking of coffee. Bershada, apparently lonesome, hung around and answered needle-workers' questions.

But of course, having come in, the curious had to buy something. Business was brisk, which almost made it worthwhile.

It got to be quarter to three. Betsy still hadn't had a chance to clean the mess in back, and she was getting really hungry. She was about to phone the deli next door to ask Jack to bring her a sandwich, when Jill came in with an aromatic paper bag. "Tomato rice soup from the Waterfront Café, which is rocking with stories of your fall from grace," she announced.

With it came half a grilled cheese sandwich, which Betsy ate first, for an immediate dose of fat and carbs. The soup came in a large round carton. Betsy declined a spoon, electing to drink it straight.

"Ah," she sighed after three big gulps. "That's better.

Jill, have you met Bershada Reynolds? She's going to be coming to Monday Bunch gatherings now she's retired. Bershada, this is Jill Cross."

"Officer Cross," said Bershada in greeting, adding to Betsy, "She's given me a traffic ticket or two."

"Around the station house we call her Miss Lead-foot," said Jill gravely.

"Well, it's hard for me to decide which of you is my brightest star," said Betsy. "One kept customers from walking off with my shop and the other kept me from dying of hunger. Thank you both."

Bershada was still laughing when she left the shop with her purchases. Jill said, "How bad was it?"

"Was? Still is. Take a look, I can't find a minute to even start picking up. It's all the fault of that one stupid shelf. It broke as soon as I took hold of it."

Betsy drank more soup while adding up the purchases of another customer. Jill came to report, "That shelf can go back up. And the urn doesn't appear to be broken. You'll need to buy more supplies, though."

"I'm glad about the urn, but I think I'll replace the shelf with something sturdier."

"No need to, really. Just use heavier nails—or better, wood screws. You can even use the same holes if you use wood screws thicker than the original nails. That way you won't have to get in there with that imitation-wood paste."

Betsy stared at her.

Jill smiled. "What? You don't know about wood paste? Or wood screws?"

"Sure I do. But Jill, you are a genius, you showed me

the way!" Betsy was so excited, she lost the thin veneer of Minnesota restraint she'd grown the past year and gave Jill a big hug.

Jill politely allowed it for a short while, then disentangled herself. "I don't understand," she said.

Betsy caught the eye of a customer over Jill's shoulder and said, "That's a DMC skein of floss you're holding, Mrs. McLean, please don't put it in with the Anchor colors." Then she leaned forward and said quietly, "Both Nancy and Ellie-Ann used the word 'nailed' when talking about the gates leading from her basement to the pet shop basement—the bookstore and pet store and gift shop are all in one building, did you know that?"

Jill nodded.

"And that there are gates between the barriers set up between the basements?"

"No, I didn't know that."

"The gates were nailed shut years and years ago, so while Paul Schmitt could have gotten into the basement of the gift shop, everybody decided he couldn't get through the pet shop basement into the bookstore basement."

"Okay."

Betsy continued, "But when I looked at the door to Ellie-Ann's basement, it's not nailed shut, it's screwed shut. And when you just now said you could put bigger screws into the nail holes, it struck me." A customer came up with a cross-stitch pattern and a fistful of DMC floss, so there was a pause while Betsy wrote up the sales slip and collected the money. Then she said,

"Don't you see? That's why Paul was 'bone dry' when Mike went to talk to him about Angela. He didn't have to go out in the rain to get to the bookstore, he went through the basement. Back then Ace Hardware was selling wood screws right across the street."

"But surely even Mike would have noticed that the screws were new."

"Oh," said Betsy, frowning. "Well, the screws I saw were rusty, but of course this happened five years ago, so they would be."

"Unless . . ." said Jill.

"Unless what?"

"If Paul was a handyman, one of those people with a shop in his basement or garage, he probably had a tin can full of old screws and nails. Lars does, and my dad did, anyone who does work around his house does."

"Paul did carpentry work well enough to get paid for it," said Betsy. "So, see? That could explain it, couldn't it? Of course it would have taken time to put those screws in. Did Mike go down in the bookstore basement right away?"

"I don't know. I wouldn't think so."

"How soon after he got to the crime scene did they go looking for Paul?"

"Not right away, I wouldn't think. In fact, I know they didn't. They still hadn't when I got there. I was called in to guard the back door, as I told you, and arrived about fifteen minutes after I was called, which was probably half an hour after Mike got there, which was probably twenty minutes after the patrol officer arrived."

178

Betsy nodded. "Plenty of time for him to screw those doors shut before they came looking for him."

Jill said, "But he wouldn't know he had that much time."

"He wouldn't need that much time. I'll bet he didn't do both doors, you know, just the one between the bookstore and the pet shop."

"You're right, that's the one Mike would go to, and if it wouldn't open, he wouldn't try the other—why should he?"

"Especially if the screws holding it shut were old and rusty. I'll bet he did the one door and hurried back upstairs. He wouldn't want to be found missing at the gift shop when they came looking for him. There was plenty of time later to go down and screw the second gate, between the pet store and the gift shop, shut. Is this enough to take to Mike, Jill?"

"He likes corroborative evidence, not just theory."

"Like what, after five years? If only there was a way to find out if he had a can of rusty screws around the place!"

Jill smiled and said, "I used to know the couple who bought his house. The man is Jack Scarles and I went to college with his sister. Even better, the wife is Paul's cousin, or second cousin. She may be able to tell you something useful."

"So the house is still standing?"

"Oh, heck, yes. Or at least it was a couple of years ago."

"Do you know them well enough to visit them and bring me along?"

"I think so. When do you want to go?"

"How about tonight, after I close up at five? When do you have to be at work?"

Jill moved out of the way so Mrs. McLean could buy her mix of DMC and Anchor floss, saying, "I'm doing the graveyard, so not until midnight. All right, I'll phone them as soon as I think up a reason."

After Mrs. McLean was out of earshot, Jill said, "So you're thinking Paul murdered Angela."

"Yes."

"So who murdered Paul?"

"I'm not sure yet," said Betsy.

Jill said, "If Foster Johns thought Paul murdered the woman he loved, he had a powerful motive to kill Paul."

"Yes, but you weren't here when we were telling ghost stories on Halloween. Comfort Leckie said she saw Paul Schmitt's ghost in the bookstore the night he was killed. She said it bent down, straightened, then disappeared. I don't think it was a ghost, I think it was Paul planting the shell casing Mike found only after a second search—after Paul was shot."

"Why would Paul go back two days later to plant a shell casing?"

"To frame someone else for the murder."

"Who?"

"Foster Johns. He made sure Foster was out of sight while he planted the casing and then set the other part of his plan in motion. I think he planned to shoot this other person and blame Foster. But after Paul lured him to his house, the person took his gun away from him and killed him instead."

"And you think you know who that person was?"

"I think it was Alex Miller."

"Why on earth would Paul want to kill Alex Miller?"

"Because he caught him kissing Angela. It was perfectly innocent, but Paul didn't think so. He went to an enormous amount of trouble destroying Alex's relationships with his father and brother, and was working on breaking up Alex and his wife when this happened. I think he hated Alex—and Alex didn't even know it until long after. I think when Paul needed another victim to complete his frame-up of Foster, he naturally thought of Alex Miller."

14

Just before closing, Morrie called. "What's this I hear?"

"Did Jill call you?" Betsy asked indignantly.

"Call me about what?"

Betsy hesitated. "Why did you call?"

"Because I heard you tried a crash landing in the back of Crewel World—which is a very appropriate name, I think—and ruined your nice red dress."

"It's not ruined. Or at least I hope not. It's soaking in cold water and Orvus. I'll wring it out later and see."

"That's good. Now, what would Jill have told me if she'd called?"

"How should I know?"

"If I may be so bold as to quote Ricky Ricardo,

'Looooo-see, what are you up to?' " Morrie did a pretty good Cuban accent.

"All right, I'm going out to visit the people who live in what was once Paul and Angela Schmitt's house. Jill's taking me."

"What do you think you'll find out there after a lapse of five years?"

"I'm not sure. Why did you call?"

"I wanted to take you out to dinner."

"Not tonight."

"Tomorrow?"

"Yes, all right. About six-thirty?"

"See you then, sweetcakes."

"God, he's nice," said Betsy, climbing into Jill's big old Buick Roadmaster an hour later.

"Who?"

"Morrie. He's taking me out to dinner tomorrow."

"Where to?"

"I didn't ask. We did Italian last time, so probably to a steakhouse."

"Has he ever cooked for you?"

"Once." Betsy chuckled. "That's when I learned why he's so thin."

They went up Water Street, away from the Excelsior Bay of Lake Minnetonka, turned right at the top onto County 19 and followed it back around until the lake came into view again.

Lake Minnetonka isn't exactly one lake. It's more an awkward sprawl of seven lakes all run together, and the little towns that once dotted its border have nowadays pretty much run together to form a single town four hundred miles long and a quarter of a mile wide.

Navarre begins a little before County Road 19 joins County Road 15. Coming up 19, a big gray board sign reads "Navarre" and under it "City of Orono." Spring Lake is around the corner on 15, with its own smaller sign (though it's actually a bigger town) announcing that it, too, is both Spring Lake and City of Orono, and at the other end of Spring Lake is Mound, City of Orono. Orono is a small city that has done on a small scale what many of its big sisters have done: grown until it engulfed its neighbors.

The streets of all three towns followed the meandering lakeshore, and were a maze of curves and dead ends. Betsy was glad Jill was driving, because in the early dark she was hopelessly confused a minute after they turned off the highway. But Jill went confidently down this street, up that street, turned onto this lane, and pulled into an asphalt driveway, up to a two-bay garage.

Peering into the dimness, Betsy saw an ordinary gray clapboard house, probably built in the 1950s as a little summer cottage. A partial second floor had been added, and a new-looking mud or utility room now connected the garage and the house. The nearest house was at least fifty yards away, and a number of mature trees obscured its shape.

"Handyman's special," remarked Jill as they went up a newly-laid brick walk and up two cement steps to the little porch, whose roof was held up by two raw timber beams.

The door frame looked new, but the window beside

it had its original and inadequate shutters. The clapboards were also original, made of wood. Jill rang the bell, which pealed in three impressive notes.

The door was opened by a very fair girl about nine years old. "Hi, Ms. Cross," she said. "Won't you come in?" She saw Betsy and added hastily, "And your friend, too."

"Is your daddy home yet?" asked Jill as she and Betsy shed coats in the small entrance hall. A narrow stairway with white balusters rose ahead of them. To their right was an open doorway leading into a sparely furnished living room.

"Yes, he's in the kitchen with Mommy making hors d'oeuvres. That's what he calls 'em, but I think they're just crackers and funny-tasting cheese." She led the way into the living room, which, Betsy saw, had a brick fireplace with a raised hearth surrounding it on three sides. A small fire was burning merrily—a gas fire, Betsy noted, licking around a pair of imitation logs.

Jill and Betsy sat on a couch facing the fireplace, and the child went to sit on the raised hearth.

"What's your name?" asked Betsy.

"Kaitlyn Marie Searles."

"How old are you?"

"I'll be ten on December fourteenth."

"How long have you lived in this house?"

Kaitlyn had to think about that. "When we moved here, I was in second grade."

"So about three years."

"I guess so."

"Do you like this house?"

"Oh, yes, it's got lots more room than our apartment. And we have a great big yard, and we have a boat and everything."

"Do you know who lived here before you?"

The child turned solemn, and nodded. She nodded toward the floor in front of the fireplace. "That's where it happened."

"What happened?" asked Jill.

Her voice fell to a very soft whisper, which she aided with elaborate mouth movements. "The murder."

"Who was murdered?" asked Jill in an interested voice, leaning forward to make a friendly conspiracy of the conversation.

"A man named Paul Schmitt. He was my mommy's cousin. This used to be his house. Someone shot him with a gun, right here in this room. Everything was washed and they even painted it before we came here, but . . ." She leaned sideways and put her finger into a big chip taken from a brick in the top row of the hearth. "See that?"

Jill and Betsy craned their necks. Jill said, "Yes, I do. Can you see it, Betsy?"

"Yes. What is it?"

"That's from a bullet."

"It is?" Jill looked very impressed.

Betsy went for a closer look. The chip was substantial. She said, "Who told you that?"

"No one," said the child. "Daddy said it is not from a bullet, but Mommy said that chip wasn't there *before*."

"Before what?"

"Just before. I think before Paul Schmitt was . . . *murdered*. Mommy used to come here to visit Paul Schmitt."

Testing, Jill asked, "Did Paul Schmitt have a wife?"

"Yes. I think she was murdered, too, only not in this house."

The child was beginning to look nervous, so Betsy said, "This looks like a nice house for pets. Do you have any?"

"Yes, we have a cat and a dog."

"Do you? I have a cat, too. I bet my cat's bigger than yours. My cat Sophie weighs twenty-three pounds." Betsy formed a shape with her hands to show the immense dimensions of Sophie.

Kaitlyn came back stoutly. "Okay, but I bet our dog is bigger than your cat. He's a chocolate Lab, except he's not real chocolate, he's just the same color as chocolate."

"If you have a grown-up Lab, he probably weighs as much as three Sophies."

That tickled Kaitlyn, and she was still laughing when her parents came into the room.

"What's so funny?" asked Mr. Searles.

"Toby weighs as much as three cats!"

"He weighs as much as six cats, you mean."

Betsy said, "I have a cat that weighs twenty-three pounds."

Mr. Searles stared at her. He was an average-size man with light brown hair surrounding a bald spot. His face was long, his eyes blue and kind. He wore relaxed-fit jeans and a green sweater. "In that case, it only takes a cat and a half that size to make one Toby."

The notion of half a cat tickled Kaitlyn even more. Her father put a tray of crackers with dollops of a melted cheese mixture on the coffee table. "Kaitlyn, go help your mother bring in the drinks."

"You're being too kind," said Betsy. "We weren't expecting to be treated like company."

He raised an eyebrow at them, meaning they should wait until Kaitlyn left the room before continuing.

Once the child was gone, he said, "She doesn't know."

Betsy said, surprised, "Doesn't know what?"

"That my wife's cousin was murdered in this house."

Betsy looked to Jill for guidance. Jill said, "Kaitlyn was showing us the chip taken out of the hearth of your fireplace the night Paul Schmitt was murdered in this room."

"Oh, jeez," he said, and dropped into an easy chair at right angles to the couch. "How much does she know?"

Betsy said, "She knows that Paul was shot to death in this room, and that his wife was murdered elsewhere. She didn't seem troubled by the murder of Paul, but instead rather thrilled by it. She does seem a bit bothered by Angela's murder."

Jill said, "That may be because she doesn't know as much about it. She may think there is something especially awful about her death, or something somehow threatening to you or Mrs. Searles."

Betsy asked, "Where are your other children?"

"Alan's at a Cub Scout meeting. Jessica is staying overnight at a neighbor's. They don't know . . ." He grimaced. "I *thought* they didn't know anything about this. But if Kaitlyn knows—she's the second oldest, and a blabbermouth—then I suspect they all know."

"How did you come to move into this house?" asked Betsy.

"My wife's mother and Paul's mother were sisters, their parents' only children. Paul's parents are divorced, and his mother is remarried and living in Ohio. We'd been trying to save for a house, but with three children, it was slow going. This house was notorious and they were having trouble finding a buyer. We put in a very low bid, they offered a contract for deed, and so far, so good."

"It looks as if you're making improvements, too," noted Jill.

"Some." Searles nodded and looked around the room. "Some were done by Paul. He tore down half a wall to put a built-in china closet in the dining room, remodeled the kitchen at least once, enlarged the garage, and installed the gas log. That last one I really appreciate. We all love a fire, but I hate chopping wood."

"About that chip on the hearth," began Betsy.

"Yes, I keep saying I'm going to replace it, but it's pretty low on the list right now. It's not a functional defect. We don't know what it's from."

"Kaitlyn said your wife said it wasn't there, quote, before, close quote."

"It wasn't there when she visited the house, or at

least she doesn't remember it," said Searles. "But she hadn't visited here for months before it happened. There wasn't any, er, that is, the place was all cleaned up when we moved in. No bloodstains, no broken furniture, nothing to show what happened here."

"No ghosts?" asked Betsy.

He gave her a funny look, but shook his head. "No one's reported anything."

"Here we are!" caroled a woman's voice, and Kaitlyn came skipping sideways ahead of her mother through a swinging door. Mrs. Searles carried a tray on which were four mugs and a steaming pitcher. The air warmed with the scent of apples, cinnamon, and cloves.

The mugs were filled and handed around. "What were you talking about before we came in?" asked Mrs. Searles.

"Little pitchers," said Searles.

"Little pictures of what?"

"The kind that have big ears," said Searles.

"Oh. Kaitlyn, Mommy and Daddy want to have some grown-up talk with these two ladies. Do you think you could give Toby a walk in the yard for a little while?"

"Okay, Mommy."

Searles made sure he heard the back door close before he explained to his wife that Kaitlyn, and probably the rest of the children, knew about Paul Schmitt's murder. "She told Jill and her friend that the chip taken out of the hearth was probably done by a stray bullet."

Jill had risen while Searles was talking and gone to

look into the fireplace. Now she stooped for a closer look at the chip.

Mrs. Searles said, "I never said anything like that to her, of course. Anyway, I thought it was done during the fight, Paul's head striking it, maybe."

Jill said, "If a man's head hit this brick hard enough to break it, there would have been no need to shoot him. I'm no expert, but this doesn't look like it was done by a bullet. There's no trace of lead, for example. And no other mark of a ricochet—were these doors new when you moved in?" Jill indicated the brass-framed glass doors of the fireplace.

"No," said Mrs. Searles. "I remember them from way back."

"Then I'd say this is from a hammer or other tool, maybe done when the gas fire was being installed."

"Really?" said Mrs. Searles. "Well, then, Bob, you're off the hook." She explained to Jill, "I've been nagging him to replace that brick, it bothered me to look at it."

Betsy said, "Do you remember visiting Paul's workshop on a visit out here?"

The woman nodded and took a sip from her mug. "Mmmmm, this came out really good! But I couldn't tell you much about his shop, I really don't know much about tools."

"What I was wondering was, did you notice that he kept old nails and screws? A lot of carpenter types do."

She frowned and took another drink while she thought. "Oh, you mean in jars? He did this clever thing where he nailed the lids to the underside of a

190

shelf and screwed the jars onto the lids. That way he could have glass jars he could see into but without the danger of knocking one over and getting broken glass all over the floor. He had nuts and bolts and nails and screws all separated in them. He was a very neat person, and clever, too."

Betsy asked, "Were the nails and screws bright and new or old and rusty?

"Both. Some were new, some were rusty."

Betsy smiled and took a deep draught of her cider. "Ummm, this *is* good!" she said.

Mrs. Searles said, "I just remembered, that chip couldn't have happened when the gas log was put in. The last time I was here, it had just been installed, and there wasn't that chip out of the brick. Angela really liked that gas log, she said something about not having to sweep the bricks anymore since they didn't have shaggy logs on the hearth, and I distinctly remember noticing how clean and smooth the hearth was. She was *such* a good housekeeper!"

On the way home, Betsy asked, "Did you mean it about that brick being chipped by a hammer, not Paul's head or a bullet?"

Jill nodded. "Yes. Or a piece of flying furniture. You know, I looked around, but didn't see any other evidence of a violent man. Maybe they patched the walls and replaced the windows."

"Was he the sort who broke things?"

"Mike Malloy said he was. They thought at first the murderer had broken down the back door to get in the house, then realized the door had been broken well before the murder. Very typical. Paul being a handyman kept rumors from being spread by a steady stream of repairmen."

"It's a good thing the Searles aren't the kind inclined to see ghosts. I think that place would give a sensitive person nightmares."

Jill smiled. "Do you believe in ghosts?"

"Sure. Don't you?"

15

Around nine the next morning Betsy was pouring a second cup of English Breakfast tea when her phone rang.

It was Foster Johns. "Have you found out anything?" he asked, hope painful in his voice.

"A few things," she replied. "For one, Paul's alibi for Angela's murder is no good anymore."

She explained and he fairly exploded with pleasure. "There! There it is! I was hoping against hope, and by God you've done it! I knew that bastard killed Angela, and now you've proved it!"

"I haven't proven anything, yet. All I've done is poke a hole in Paul Schmitt's alibi."

"Have you talked to the police about this?"

"Not yet. Sergeant Malloy isn't fond of amateur sleuths, though he hasn't ordered me not to investigate. He's even hoping I'll prove you did it."

"Let him hope," growled Foster. "What next?"

"I want to ask you something. Do you know Alex Miller? You went to school with him."

"Well, I remember him. Haven't seen him in a long time. Years. He has a brother who last I heard works with his father in his auto shop; his name's Jory."

"Yes, that's right, I talked with Jory and his father, and I've talked with Alex. Did you know both brothers?"

"You bet. They're a year apart, Alex and Jory, but they hung out together so much, people thought they were twins. They each bought a beater car in high school, and they were always swapping parts, trying to keep them running. After a while, I don't think they knew which car was whose, there were so many parts from each car on the other." Foster was chuckling at the memory.

"Do you remember that Paul Schmitt was also friends with Alex and Jory?"

That put an end to the laughter. Betsy could hear Foster drawing a long, be-patient breath. "Yes, I do remember that. Actually, we were all friends back then, Paul, Alex, Jory, and me. And three other guys, Max, Mark and Mike, the 3M Company, they hung out with us sometimes, too. We played softball, went to Twins games, pulled practical jokes on each other, talked about cars and girls."

"Did Paul strike you back then as the jealous kind?"

"No, not particularly. But we didn't pair off like the kids do today, getting serious in sixth grade. Dating was casual for most of us; in fact, I don't remember that Paul had a real girlfriend at all, until he met

Angela. And that was in college."

"Do you remember Paul getting angry with any of you?"

"Well, yes. Not viciously angry, not enough to quit hanging out with us altogether. He'd be sore for a day, then pull some kind of prank, you know, a practical joke, and we'd all laugh at the poor sucker he'd done it to, and we'd be friends again. Well, except one time he really set up the 3M boys. I don't remember all the details, it was kind of complicated, but Mike ended up on suspension and Max actually transferred to another school. Mike blamed Max, but Paul told us later he rigged the whole thing—whatever it was. I thought at the time Paul started something that turned into more than he meant it to. I do know he ran quiet the rest of the semester."

When Betsy went down to open up, there was yet again a figure standing in the doorway, this time a Minnesota-style Valkyrie, a tall, sturdy guardian of lives and property. But this one wore her armor under her shirt and carried her weapon in a holster. In other words, Jill.

Betsy hurried to unlock the door. "Did you talk to Malloy? What did you find out?" she asked.

"Mike says he checked the gate in the bookstore basement. He says it was fastened shut and so he didn't feel a need to check the other gate. He recalls being told by the owner of the building that the gates were nailed shut in 1973. Note once again the use of the word 'nailed.' But he says it's possible that Paul's alibi can be considered broken."

Betsy said, "That's good, that's great! Anything else?"

"Not much. I read the report on Paul Schmitt's murder."

"What time did it happen?"

"The 911 call came in at nine twenty-seven."

"Okay, Alex works second shift now, but maybe he was working graveyard or first shift back then. Can you find out?"

"If I call up there, they'll want to know who I am. When I say Officer Jill Cross, they'll want to know why I'm asking, and what can I say? I'm not an investigator, I'm not doing it because a supervisor asked me to."

"Jill—"

"No. You want to know, you ask." Jill wasn't speaking sharply, she didn't even look annoyed. But her cool, Gibson-girl face gave Betsy no hope at all.

"Turn the radio on for me, will you?" Betsy asked, and went to the checkout desk to haul a phone book out of a bottom drawer. She found the number of the Ford plant and dialed it. She said to the person who answered using her most brisk and impersonal tone, "Personnel, please." When a man from personnel got on the wire, Betsy said in the same voice, "I need a confirmation of employment for one Alexander Miller, please." This was the term credit card people used when they asked Betsy about her employees.

There was a pause while computer keys rattled faintly. "Yes, he's our second shift engine assembly line supervisor," reported the man in personnel.

"How long has he worked for you?" asked Betsy.

"Hmmm, twelve years."

"Always second shift?"

"Why do you ask?"

Betsy allowed her voice to soften. "Well, I've got a cousin who's working first shift and he has an idea he'd like to try second, now he and his wife have a baby. This way, they don't have to put him in day care. But I was wondering if people who work second shift stay with it. I mean, the hours are screwy, you're trying to sleep when everyone else is up, and so on."

She looked over and saw Jill staring at her with raised eyebrows, and looked away again, lest she start laughing.

The personnel manager said, "Well, I've never worked second shift, but Mr. Miller has been on it for seven years."

"Is he late a lot, or taking a lot of sick leave? I mean, Will is very reliable and all, but I'm wondering if that might change."

"I don't think checking just one record is going to help you much, you know."

"You know, you're right. I shouldn't be asking you all this, anyhow. His wife asked me for advice and I don't know what to tell her. He says the pay is better if he'll move to second shift, and they could really use the money."

The manager sighed. "Tell me about it. And for what it's worth, Miller takes all his vacation in one lump every December and he hasn't been late or off sick since he started that shift."

"Say, that's very encouraging." Betsy resumed her brisk voice. "Thank you very much. Good-bye and have a nice day." She hung up.

Jill, leaning against the box shelves that divided the counted cross-stitch back of the shop from the knitting and needlepoint front, said, "Girl, I had no idea you were such a con artist."

"Well, what else could I do? You wouldn't help me!"

"I take it the news is bad."

"Not for him. He was at work the night Paul was murdered."

"Ah. Too bad."

"Yeah."

"You're back to Foster, then."

"Yeah." Betsy opened the cash register and began to put the opening-up paper and silver into the drawer. "Alex did tell me he didn't know what Paul was doing to him until after Paul had been dead a while. I was hoping he was lying." She mulled that setback over while the soft airs of something classical played on the radio. Then she asked, "Do you know where Comfort Leckie lives?"

"No, why?"

"I want to ask her something."

Jill murmured, "Bulldog, bulldog, rah, rah, rah."

"What?"

"Just glad you're not quitting. I'm sure she's in the phone book, why don't you call her?"

"All right, in a while."

Jill, smiling, said, "How about I buy you lunch in a

couple of hours? You can tell me all about it."

Betsy laughed. "All right. But it's my turn to buy."

"Comfort, it's Betsy Devonshire."

"Hello, Betsy. What's up?"

"I was thinking about your story of seeing Paul's ghost in the bookstore. Do you know about what time of the evening that was?"

"Let me think. It was such a long time ago . . ."

Betsy waited patiently, and at last Comfort said, "Near as I can remember, it was after six-thirty. It was dark—real dark, not the dark you get when the weather is bad, but I don't think it was as late as seven. It was windy, the wind turned my umbrella inside out. It was sleeting hard and had been for a while, there was slush on the streets and sidewalks. Is that what you wanted to know?"

"Yes, that's it. Thanks, Comfort."

"I take it you'll explain that question one of these days."

"I sure hope so. Bye."

"May I special-order the linen?" Mrs. Hubert asked Godwin. She had just paid for several Marc Saastad iris patterns—she grew varieties of iris in her beautiful front yard, and the Saastad patterns were very accurate about varieties—and the expensive silks to stitch them. But Crewel World didn't have the high-count linen in the shade of green she wanted.

Godwin considered that. Special orders were a special pain for a small business. It cost twice as much per yard to order a small piece as it did to order five or more yards, plus there was the rapid-delivery cost, and of course the customer grudged the difference—and only too often found the fabric at another store before the special order arrived, or changed her mind altogether about the project.

"Can you pay in advance?" asked Godwin.

Now it was the customer's turn to consider the problems with that. "How much?" she asked after a pause. Godwin had already calculated the add-on charges, and named a price that included a small profit.

"I'll write you a check—can you get it before the fifteenth of November? We're leaving for Florida the twentieth."

"Certainly. I'll call Norden Crafts today." Godwin wrote up the order and phoned it in as soon as Mrs. Hubert left. He bantered a bit with salesman/owner Dave Stott and, so long as he had him on the line, placed another order for three more Kwanzaa patterns. Stott reported the linen was in stock, and said he might be able to get it in the mail yet today.

The door went *Bing!* a few minutes later, and so did Godwin's heart when he saw the incredibly handsome Rik Lightfoot come in.

"Hi," said Rik in his rich voice.

"Hi," said Godwin, batting his eyelashes furiously. "May I help you, I really, really hope?"

Rik laughed. "Down, boy, I'm heterosexual. I thought I had enough Anchor 308 for that lab pattern, but it turns out I don't." He went to the wooden cabinet and ran a forefinger down the sets of shallow drawers

199

until he found the deep golden brown he was looking for. He bought two skeins and said, "Where's the lady who was behind the counter last time I came in?"

"She's at lunch. She's heterosexual, too."

Rik laughed and Godwin thought he'd melt right into his penny loafers.

"Is it true that the best bass fishing in the state is right here in Lake Minnetonka?" asked Rik.

"I've heard that," hazarded Godwin, who didn't know one of the biggest bass fishing tournaments in the country was held on the lake every year.

"Can people fish off the docks here?"

"Sure," said Godwin, who had no idea at all if that were true.

"I want to see if a technique I learned in Montana works here. You see, you skip your jig sideways so it goes under the dock, where fish hang out in the shadow of the boards, just like they hide around sunken logs or under water lilies." Rik made a sideways casting gesture and Godwin melted all over again at the display of shoulder and back.

"You make it sound really interesting," said Godwin fervently, leaning on the desk to get just a little closer to the man.

"Well, Minnesota makes a lot of famous lures, and with all those lakes, I should think just about everyone here likes to fish."

"Oh, I agree with that," nodded Godwin without mentioning he was an exception.

"It must be nice, living right on the shore of such a great lake."

"I love to go out on the water," said Godwin. "I get out there whenever I can in the summer."

"Of course, Mille Lacs is good, too," continued Rik.

"That's what I hear," said Godwin, whose only trip to that lake was to visit an Indian casino.

"Nothing like a fresh walleye. The best I ever had I caught in a Canadian lake that didn't even have a road to it, we had to fly in. Caught my limit in less than an hour. Used a spoon. Dropped it . . ." Again Rik made a casting gesture, this time forward, toward the door. "I barely started to reel it in when all of a sudden, *bam,* he hit that line and took off with it. I thought I was gonna lose him, he ran right up along the shore, wound himself around tree roots, practically buried himself in some big rocks. But I just set the reel and let him go, and pretty soon he came right back at me, and five minutes later he came alongside the boat, tame as a kitten, practically asking me to take him out of the water."

"How . . . interesting," said Godwin, a little desperately.

"I tell you, after eating those fillets, I just about swore off fishing back in the States. But it's the sport that draws me, I do a lot of catch and release now."

"I suppose that happens a lot," said Godwin. "I mean to people who have eaten walleye fillets, er, caught with a spoon in Canada."

Rik, enlightened, laughed. "Yes, you're right. Well, thanks for an interesting conversation—what's your name?"

"Godwin DuLac. Nice to meet you. Come back again

when you need anything in the needle arts line."

He watched Rik go with a little sigh, and when Betsy came back from lunch, he announced that he had saved her from a terrible fate: having to listen to fish talk. "I tell you, I thought that man was perfect, he is *so* handsome and he does needlework and he drives a *Porsche,* for heaven's sake. But he not only fishes, he *loves* to talk about it. Do you know what he told me? He said he fishes with a spoon! Is that possible? Or did he see my eyes glazing over and start to spoof me?"

"There's a kind of fishing lure called a spoon," said Betsy, laughing at his woebegone expression. "So I take it he is gay?"

"Oh. Well, no, he said he was heterosexual when he heard me panting at his approach. But if you are wise, Betsy, when he comes in again, run for the back room or he'll start teaching you how to cast under a dock."

"All right," lied Betsy, who used to love to fish. "Anything else interesting happen while I was gone?"

"Well, I sold a set of Kwanzaa patterns, that's the third set, so I told Dave to send us three more. And—I hope you aren't angry about this, but I took a special order. I know you don't like them, but it's for Mrs. Hubert, and she bought all the silks as well as the patterns for three Saastad irises, plus she paid in advance." He held out the order.

"And she agreed to pay a premium for the fabric, so it's all right," said Betsy, looking at it. "But before it happens again, I want to try something Susan Greening Davis suggested, and call some other shops to see if we can't order some of this less popular stuff together. If I can get three others to go in with me, the order will be big enough to get a price break."

"But you don't have room for more fabric on your shelves," warned Godwin. "And you're already storing stock in the bathroom."

"I know. Goddy, do you think it would be a good idea to set up some storage shelves in the basement? I was thinking of moving all the household stuff out of there and putting the stock in that back room into the basement. I nearly broke my neck yesterday trying to reach that top shelf."

"I know. But if you start thinking you've got lots of storage room, next thing you know, you'll have way too much money tied up in stock."

"Hmmm." That was a good point. The temptation was to carry items no one else did. What fun it would be placing an order for some of the real exotica! But the intelligent way to offer a wider range of products was to expand, to move the deli or the bookstore out and take over the space, so the stock could be out on shelves for her customers to see and be tempted by. On the other hand, she was barely making ends meet in the needlework shop right now, while Jack and Fort were paying their rent every single month. Could she afford to take a big hit while her expanded store got on its feet? Not really. Maybe she should work harder on getting the present Crewel World farther into the black before considering expansion.

Of course, having made that decision, the next two customers each wanted uncommon patterns Betsy didn't carry. The idea of expansion remained a flickering hope in the recesses of her heart.

"Where are we going?" asked Betsy that evening, as Morrie handed her up into his big Wagoneer.

"A place called Thanh Do."

"Vietnamese food." Betsy nodded, pleased. She had changed into a royal blue dress he liked on her because, he said, it showed how blue her eyes were. She carried a delicate shawl a shade lighter than the dress in case of drafts, but wore her heavy winter coat for the journey because the forecast was for temperatures to drop below thirty.

He got in on his side and said, "Not just Vietnamese, they do all kinds of Asian food. It's becoming very popular, and I think you'll like it." A true Minnesotan, he just wore a sweater-vest under a wool sports coat.

They drove up Highway 7 to just past Knollwood Mall in St. Louis Park, turned left on Texas and went to Minnetonka, left again and almost immediately turned into a parking lot beside a dry cleaners. The parking lot was narrow but deep and behind the dry cleaners was a two-window storefront with a modest green sign. "Thanh Do," it read, the *A* formed by a pair of red chopsticks. A red hibiscus bloomed in one window.

Morrie had made it sound fancier than this, but she didn't say anything—he was very reliable about restaurants.

They alighted and went in. A significant portion of the floor space was taken up by a life-size gray stone statue of Buddha as a slim young man surrounded by plants and bamboo. A table or altar with lit candles stood in front of the statue and a fat sitting Buddha was on it. The air was fragrant not only with the usual "Chinese restaurant" smells of hot sugar, garlic, ginger and meat, but also of herbs.

A waiter with blond hair and delicate metal earrings took them to a black Naugahyde booth in back. He left them with big ivory-colored menus that noted that all meals were cooked from scratch with fresh ingredients, so customers were asked to be patient.

"What do you recommend?" asked Betsy.

"Well, do you like seafood?"

"Yes, but only on the coasts, where it's fresh. Why?"

"Never mind."

Betsy looked and found the item he was hinting about, a teriyaki dish for two called Pacific Blue, containing shrimp, scallops, squid, salmon, and yellow-fin tuna on a bed of steamed vegetables and wood mushrooms. A pair of asterisks warned it was spicy. She was tempted, but the herb-scented air made her decide on single-asterisk Vietnamese basil chicken. Morrie chose a triple-asterisk curry dish and asked them to bump it up to four stars. She ordered a Chinese beer, Morrie a Beck's Dark.

"So how's the sleuthing coming along?" Morrie asked while they waited for their food.

"Paul murdered Angela, and I think I've figured out how."

"Tell me."

"You know he worked in that gift shop called Heritage II, on the corner of Second and Water?"

Morrie nodded.

"Well, Heritage and the pet shop next door and the bookstore next to that are all in one building, with a single basement."

Morrie's eyebrows rose. "You don't mean Sergeant Malloy doesn't know that."

"No, he knows it, he even checked on it right away. But there are board walls dividing the basement space according to the shop space overhead, and while there used to be gates between them, they were nailed shut years before the murder took place."

"Ah," nodded Morrie. "But you think . . . ?"

"Well, first of all, I thought it was odd he didn't come out to see what the commotion was about when the window of the bookstore was broken. After all, he took that job to keep an eye on Angela, so he'd be sensitive to anything happening outside and nearby. Even a thunderstorm doesn't make a racket every minute, and he should have at least heard the sirens. I think he didn't come out because he had to stay dry, so his alibi would work.

"You think he came through the basement spaces?"

"Yes. It's true, people will tell you, that these gates were nailed shut many years ago. However, if you go look at them, they are *screwed* shut."

"Screwed, nailed, what's the difference?"

"I think Paul concluded some while before the murder that Angela and Foster were in love, and that's why he decided to murder her. Then he waited for several things to come together. One was the storm. Rain or snow, it didn't matter, but it had to be wet out. I think he pulled the nails on those gates so he could get through to the bookstore, so he'd be bone dry when Mike Malloy went to talk to him after Angela was shot. It's possible he put the screws in, just in case someone tugged on the gates, but when conditions were right, he unscrewed them. It was Angela's night to close up, she was alone in the store. Foster had come by to wave at her. Paul went down through the basements, up into the bookstore, and shot Angela. On his way back, Paul screwed the bookstore gate shut—no sound of hammering, by the way—then went down late that night or the next day and screwed the gate between the pet shop and the gift shop closed. He used rusty screws he brought from home—I have a witness who saw the jars of screws in his workshop. His cousin, who now lives in his house, described how he kept a very neat shop, with new and rusty old screws and nails and such kept in separate jars."

The waiter brought their beer and frosty glasses and Morrie poured his professionally, down the inside of the glass, so it wouldn't form a big head. "I take it you've looked at the gates?"

"I looked in the pet store basement and in the bookstore basement. They are screws, not nails; they have that slot in the head. They're on the pet store side of the gate to the bookstore."

Morrie looked interested. "And are there, by chance, nail holes beside the screws?"

"No."

He winced with regret at scoring a point and looked away.

"But," said Betsy, "I had a shelf fall down in my shop the other day, and Jill told me to use wood screws a size bigger and put them in the nail holes when I put it back up. Paul Schmitt was a good amateur carpenter, he would surely think of that. And, since he used old screws, they weren't shiny new when Mike went to take a look at the gate. This isn't proof he murdered his wife, but you see how his alibi isn't worth spit anymore."

Morrie thought that over for a few moments. "Well, all right, you're right," he said. "How did you get the idea to go exploring in the basement, anyhow?"

She told him about the search for Iams, adding, "If you go down there today, you'll see the pet store has lined both walls with metal shelves crowded with stock—but that happened *after* the murder of Angela. But I'm not sure if I should go to Mike yet. What do you think?"

"Do you think he'll listen to you?"

"Maybe. I don't know. Maybe not. I wish I could convince him I'm just another informant. I'm sure he has informants."

Morrie grinned. "If you want to be an informant, you'll have to make him pay you for your information."

She laughed. "That's what my problem is, I've been giving him information for nothing, and he values it accordingly."

"What else have you found out?"

"I thought I had come up with an alternative to Foster for Paul's murder, but it turned out he has a really good alibi, given by a time clock." She told the story of Alex Miller's claim of a plot by Paul to ruin his life, and how she'd found out he was at work at the critical time. "So I guess Alex is in the clear, his alibi seems solid."

Morrie said, "But was Alex right about Paul's sabotage? That sounds a little elaborate for someone who isn't operating in a James Bond novel."

"Well, his middle school teacher remembers that Paul was a born genius at setting others up to take the blame for something he'd done, or getting them to do something against the rules; and Jory remembers Paul loving practical jokes, one of which involved injuring a cat. So that's why I'm thinking that Paul was killed while trying to frame someone else for Angela's murder."

"How?"

"Comfort Leckie saw his ghost in the bookstore the night he was murdered."

He stared at her. "Ghost? You're not going to tell me you believe in ghosts!"

"Of course I do, I've seen them myself. But listen to this." She repeated the story Comfort had told of seeing Paul's ghost in the bookstore.

"You think Paul's *ghost* planted evidence of some sort?"

"No, no. I think the living Paul did, and Comfort saw him doing it."

Distracted, Morrie asked, "What kind of a name is Comfort, anyhow?"

"It's an old pilgrim name, handed down since the

seventeenth century to every other generation of women in her family. She's miffed none of her daughters gave it to one of their daughters. But that's beside the point. Comfort saw Paul *before* he was murdered, and what he was doing was planting the second shell casing. Mike didn't find the first one, you know. It went behind a shelf and wasn't found until they took the shelf down to replace it."

"Maybe she didn't see Paul at all, maybe she saw her own reflection in the window. People do that, and call 911 to report prowlers."

"That isn't what happened here. He turned sideways and she recognized him. The Monday Bunch thinks it's a ghost, and they're all moonstruck about it, saying Paul must have been very deeply in love with Angela."

"But you think . . . ?"

"Can you be married to someone you're stalking? He tracked her every movement, he even took that job at the gift shop so he could keep an eye on her at work in the bookstore."

"I see."

Betsy took a drink of beer and went on, "Mike Malloy searched the bookstore after Angela's murder and concluded she'd been shot with a revolver because he didn't find a shell casing. But there were shell casings in Paul's living room, and the bullets were the same caliber, so Mike went back to search the bookstore again, and this time he found a casing. Obviously, Paul planted it. Comfort saw him doing it."

He hid a smile behind a big, thin hand. "Hon, you don't even know it was him in the shop."

"Yes, I do. Comfort didn't think she was seeing a ghost, remember. She recognized Paul and wondered what he was doing in the bookstore. It was only later, when she heard about the murder, that she decided it was his ghost. And I'll tell you something else: I talked with Mike the other day and he said both casings came from the same kind of gun and they all have marks on them that make him pretty sure they were shot out of the same gun."

He sat back, defeated but still smiling. "All right, *mo chroide*." Morrie called Betsy by different endearments, trying to find one they both liked. "But why did Paul Schmitt want the cops to know the same gun was used in both murders?"

"Because he was going to frame Foster Johns for the murder of his wife."

"How?"

"I think he was going to shoot someone else with the gun he used to kill Angela, and since the bullet from Angela's murder had gone flying out the window, he needed the shell casing for them to compare. But Mike couldn't find the bookstore shell casing. So he fired the gun and went to plant a new shell casing."

"But he didn't shoot someone else, someone else shot him."

"Come on," said Betsy, "he didn't know he was going to end up dead! I think he arranged for Foster to be alone in his office that night so he'd have no alibi. Then he invited another person to come over to his house. I think the plan was to take that person to Foster's building, murder him there, and leave the gun for the police to find."

"Or her," corrected Morrie gently. "Maybe he planned to murder another woman."

"No, only a man could win a knock-down battle with Paul. Because that's what happened. He got into a fight and the person took his gun, shot him, and ran away."

"Who was this person?"

Betsy grimaced. "Since it's not Alex Miller, I don't know."

"Well, consider this. Maybe the person Paul planned to murder was Foster. Maybe Foster's lying about Paul telling him to wait in Foster's office. It's not a very good alibi, you know. I'm sure Foster could have faked it."

"I know." She lifted and set down her beer bottle on the white paper table covering, making a series of overlapping circles. "I've been thinking the person who fought with Paul was Foster Johns. Except . . ."

"Except what?"

"I just don't think he did it."

This time he didn't bother to hide his smile.

"Don't laugh at me," she protested, but she was making a rueful, amused face herself.

"I wouldn't dream of laughing at you, not with your record," he said. "But I was thinking what my boss would say if I came to him and said I didn't want to press an investigation because I had a feeling the suspect didn't do it."

"But surely you get feelings about suspects!"

"Sure I do. Often. Sometimes I'm sure a suspect did it, and sometimes I'm equally sure a suspect didn't.

Sometimes I'm right. But those feelings are more than instinct, they come from experience. You haven't been at this long enough to learn if your feelings are always right."

"I know," she sighed, sitting back in her padded seat. "But Foster Johns was so careful and, and *scrupulous* over putting that new roof on my building. I talked with the city inspector about him, and he said Foster Johns has a reputation all over the state for honest dealings. He follows the rules, he said, he insists on an independent inspector, and he only hires sub-contractors who agree to do things over if they aren't perfect. How could someone as honest as that be a murderer?"

"Well," said Morrie, leaning back in his own seat, "if I did something horribly against the law and wanted to get away with it, I'd obey the laws and follow the rules and mind even Miss Manners forever after."

"Hmmmm," conceded Betsy, turning her beer bottle around by the neck to draw a wavy line through her circles. "A middle school teacher, now retired, came to the shop the other day and told me about Paul, Jory, and Foster, all of whom she taught English. She kept diaries of her classroom days and recalled Foster as an impatient, aggressive seventh grader. He certainly is none of those things today."

Her expression was troubled, and he said, "Look, dear heart, your interest in crime is not so much to discover the culprit as to see justice done, right?"

Betsy nodded.

"Well, perhaps it already has. If Paul Schmitt murdered Angela and tried to frame Foster Johns for it, and

Foster killed him, then the scales are in balance. Perhaps you should withdraw from this one. If justice is your game, then Mum should be your name. Go home and tell no one what you've found out." He made a little motion in front of his mouth, as if turning a key. "Tick-a-lock!" he said. "Look, here comes our dinner."

16

Thanh Do's Vietnamese basil chicken was so fabulously delicious that Betsy couldn't do anything but make delighted little humming noises for a while. There were big pieces of fresh Asian basil strewn among the chicken tenders, and pineapple chunks and streamers of sweet onions in a delectable brown teriyaki sauce.

Morrie had to stop and blow his nose after every three bites of his fiery curry, which was making Betsy's eyes water clear across the table.

"Where did you learn to like food that hot?" Betsy asked when she was able to form a thought that didn't have the word "basil" in it. "Certainly not here in Minnesota, which thinks a dash of fresh-ground pepper is going wild."

Morrie nodded. "My first wife and I used to vacation in Texas every winter for about ten years. Their Tex-Mex food is wonderful, but hot enough to melt horseshoes. I actually tried to wrangle a job down there, with Houston PD, but didn't succeed."

"I'm glad," said Betsy.

"Me, too, now." He smiled at her in a way that made her heart turn over.

"Do you always fall in love this easy?" she asked.

"No. You?"

"Oh, gosh, yes."

He stopped eating to stare at her, and very slowly his face began to change, from surprise to disappointment, to sorrow, to deep, deep sorrow.

At first embarrassed, she soon began to giggle. He heaved a despairing sigh, incandescent with curry, and she became helpless with laughter.

When he pulled a handkerchief from his pocket to touch his eyes, she lay down sideways on the seat, and there, unable to see his brokenhearted face, she regained control. "Are you finished?" she asked from that position.

"Yes," he replied in a voice with a sad catch in it. "Sit up, people are staring."

She came up to see him eating his dinner with a satisfied smirk. "Idiot," she said.

"Tell me a ghost story," he said.

She told the one about Cecil's ghost haunting the house his granddaughter owns. "When the house was being remodeled to accommodate a wheelchair, Cecil would steal tools, slam doors, and wreak some kind of breakdown on the man's pickup . . ." She stopped suddenly to think.

"What?"

"I wonder how long ago it was that that happened."

"Why, is that important?"

"Probably not, but wouldn't it be strange if the carpenter was Foster Johns? He started out as a carpenter, then got into construction, and is now a general contractor."

"Are you thinking that these women played a trick on Foster?"

"No, no, nothing like that. This is a small town, and so there are lots of connections among people. Carol and Sue have been living together for sixteen years. Carol didn't say the carpenter's name. That's kind of sad, isn't it? She has this wonderful story, but she can't say it involves Foster Johns without spoiling it."

"Tell me another ghost story."

"Just let me finish this little bit here first," said Betsy, and ate some more. She was disobeying the rule slender women follow: Eat only until you're not hungry anymore. But she wasn't slender—and obviously the maker of that rule had never eaten Thanh Do's Vietnamese basil chicken. "Is everything here as good as this?"

"I haven't been disappointed yet."

"Your turn, tell me a ghost story now," she said.

"I don't know any ghost stories. But you said you've actually seen a ghost, so tell me about that."

"The bright and good one, or the scary one?"

He considered. "The scary one."

"We were camping, my parents and my sister and I. I think I was eight or nine years old. I don't know where we went, it wasn't a campground with a building that sold ice and soft drinks and charcoal starter, but a forest with no road into it, or even trails. We drove for hours, it seemed like, and arrived near sundown, and had to walk back in for a long time, carrying things. We came to a clearing in the woods and put up the tents by lamplight. I remember there were owls, two owls, hooting back and forth. Dad dug a shallow hole and we built a wood fire in it and we roasted weenies and marshmallows. He and Mama talked about themselves as children, and what school was like and what they did for fun. Mama said a favorite thing was to take an old wallet and put green paper in it so it looked nice and fat with money, and put a rubber band around it and tie a length of button thread to it and put it on the sidewalk, and when someone would reach for it, yank it back, then laugh like anything. She laughed again when she told us about it." Betsy shrugged.

"Every generation has its own sense of humor. Have you noticed that cartoons aren't funny anymore?"

Betsy said, "Boy, are you right! If I want to enjoy a cartoon, I have to wait for the Bugs and Daffy Hour."

"That wasn't much of a ghost story," said Morrie.

"I hadn't gotten to the ghost part yet. Let's see, oh, yes, parents' stories about their childhood. Well, Dad told about a brown-and-white pinto pony his father had as a boy that would rear up and strike at anyone who came near with a saddle. Only Granddad could ride it, and he had to ride bareback. It was a menace in the barn, sneaking a bite if someone got within reach of it. Except it loved Granddad and never bit him. That night I went to bed simply wild to have a pony of my own that no one but me could ride."

"Still no ghost," noted Morrie.

"Be patient, my dear. We had two tents, one for our parents, one for Margot and me. I woke up very early the next morning, convinced I'd heard a pony neighing not far away. I was absolutely positive that pony was white with big brown patches and that it would let me ride it. So I got out of my sleeping bag, put on jeans, T-shirt, and sandals, and went out looking for it. I listened and heard it neigh again, and started for it. Every time I'd get discouraged, I'd hear it again, and pretty soon I was a long way from the camp. I kept thinking about how much fun it would be to come back to the camp riding my spotted pony, which I felt I pretty much had to do, because I remembered my parents had warned me not to leave the camp alone, so I needed a spectacular excuse.

"At last I came to a meadow, but it wasn't the one we'd parked the car in the night before. And there wasn't a beautiful brown-and-white pony grazing in it, either.

"It was about then it stopped neighing, so I decided it had been a ghost pony, haunting the meadow and crying for its old owner to come play with it again.

"But I'd been wandering the woods for so long, I didn't know where I was or which way back to the camp. I started walking aimlessly, got into some brambles, and fell a few times. Some mosquitoes found me, and invited all their friends and relations to come and feast. The woods seemed dark after the sunny meadow, and I started to feel afraid. I couldn't find the tents. I just kept walking and crying and even praying. Then I saw a big box turtle. I loved turtles, so I knelt down and stroked it and cried some more, because I was really scared and getting very hungry. And so long as I was down there, I prayed really hard, and when I stood up, there was the camp on the other side of some bushes, not twenty yards away.

"I came running into camp bawling and woke everyone up. It was only about seven-thirty, I must have gotten up before six. My mother wanted to know why on earth I went off into the woods like that, and I told them about the pony, and Dad said there wasn't a horse or a pony for miles."

"How did he know?"

"He didn't say, but I'm sure we didn't just pull off the road and go camping in some stranger's woods," said Betsy. "He must have known the area."

"Still . . ." Morrie looked skeptical.

Betsy sniffed loftily. "I told the story of that ghost pony at camp, and it was very well received."

Morrie laughed. "You made that up! Well done!"

"The getting lost part wasn't made up," said Betsy. "Once when we went camping, I went out for an early-morning walk and got lost and stooped to play with a box turtle, and when I stood up, there were the tents. When I told that story in camp, I added the ghost pony and said I went out later looking for proof of the pony and guess what I found?"

Morrie said solemnly, "Horsefeathers!"

That set Betsy off into another peal of laughter. "I wish I'd thought of that when I told that story!" she said when she was able to speak again. "The best I could do was to say I found an old, rusty horseshoe just the right size for a pony's hoof."

The waiter came by. "Do you want to take that home in a box?" he asked, looking at the platter, which was still nearly half full.

"All right, thank you," said Betsy.

She was quiet on the ride home.

"A penny for that thought," Morrie said at last.

"Something . . . I said something, or you said something that triggered something, only I can't think what it is."

"Sleep on it. If you're like me, it'll come to you in a dream."

Betsy didn't know who the grinning bad man was, but he had a gun and he was going to shoot her if she didn't give him forty thousand dollars. She didn't have any money and went out on the street to look for some. And there on the sidewalk was a fat billfold full of money, but every time she stooped to reach for it, it leaped away. She finally threw herself down and grabbed it with both hands, but it resisted and finally worked itself loose from her fingers, as if it were attached to something by a rubber band.

She woke up to find herself sleeping on her belly, crosswise on the bed, one arm reaching out. "Maybe I should have tried the curry instead of eating all that basil," she muttered, straightening herself around, pulling the sheet and blanket back into place. She pushed the little button on her watch, whose face obediently lit up. Four o'clock. She had another hour and a half to sleep—today was early-bird water aerobics day. She rubbed her forehead and composed herself for sleep.

No good. She got up, grumbling.

The stupid dream had her wide awake.

Sophie, wondering what she was doing awake at such an hour, came to ask if, so long as they were up, perhaps Betsy could give her loyal, loving cat a little snack? "Not a chance," Betsy told the cat. "If I feed you now at"—she checked her watch—"four ten A.M., my God, then when I do get up at five-thirty because it's Friday and I have early-bird water aerobics, you'll have very conveniently forgotten all about this, and want your breakfast. Again. It may also cause you to decide this is customary, rising at four to feed the cat. But it isn't, so I won't. Now, go to your basket and take a nap. Shoo."

Having after countless lessons learned that Betsy could not be cajoled away from *no* when it came to food, the animal did as she was told; except she didn't take a nap, but leaned on one elbow to stare at Betsy with her yellow eyes at half mast, thinking resentful, self-pitying thoughts.

Betsy ignored her and sat down in an easy chair, turned on the standard lamp that stood behind it, and reached for her knitting, which lived in a big, bowl-shaped basket beside the chair. She had three projects under way and, considering the tired state of her mind, picked the easiest one, a thin blanket meant to be sent to Africa, part of a program her church was sponsoring. She was using an inexpensive acrylic yarn, not because she was cheap but because it could stand repeated washing, even in very hot water. There was no complexity to the stitchery, just knit and knit and knit—though she was changing colors every eight inches. But that was more to keep herself from being totally bored than to provide something a little less plain for the unfortunate individual who would sleep under it.

It took a great many stitches to get a width sufficient for even a narrow blanket, and even the promise of a change from mint green to tangerine in another three inches didn't help all that much. Betsy could knit much faster now than she could a year ago, but she was not yet up to a speed that would impress anyone but a beginner. The blanket was growing very slowly.

But after a few minutes she stopped noticing how slowly the work was progressing and fell into a state that was almost like meditation. Giving her hands something to do stopped that little voice that recited a list of things she should be doing: cleaning the bathroom, dusting, updating the books, reviewing her investments—she had an appointment with Mr. Penberthy next week, and he could always tell when she had merely glanced at them. That little voice was silent now because she *was* doing something.

On the other hand, what she was doing took about seven of her brain cells, which freed the rest to wander around and inspect the newest information she had logged into her head.

Funny how everyone had thought Paul killed himself when they first heard about his death. Jory had said Paul looked sick with sorrow over his wife's murder.

Even if Paul had been obsessed rather than in love, it must have been terrible for him to have lost her.

And that would be true even if he had murdered her. Because if he had murdered her, it was because he thought he had already lost her, to another man.

So it would make sense for him to have committed suicide.

That was the ugly pattern in so many cases, a man kills his estranged wife, and then himself. Betsy thrust the needles angrily for a few stitches. What a stupid thing, that "take her with me" syndrome! Where did they think they were going? Were they suddenly some kind of pagan, thinking that in the afterlife she would be a loving spouse again?

But in Paul's case the evidence was clear, it wasn't murder-suicide. Paul may have murdered Angela, but someone else had killed him. Who? Someone he had planned to kill, who turned the tables and killed him? Then why not come forward? Fear of arrest? People didn't go to jail for killing in self-defense.

Suppose Paul had been planning to murder Foster, and make it look like suicide. Had it been Foster at the Schmitt house? Was Treeny Larson right when she said it took only a few minutes to pull out those blueprints and papers to make it look as if Foster had been working for hours? Had Malloy gone over the papers, or had someone who really understood them looked them over, to see if they were merely random papers?

Foster Johns was happy because Betsy had broken Paul Schmitt's alibi. Betsy wondered if it was possible to prove that Paul had replaced the nails with screws.

Perhaps, if the nails had been significantly longer than the screws. There would be a tell-tale hole that went past the end of the screw. She would have to tell Jill about that.

Rik Lightfoot was a bore about fishing, Godwin said. Betsy hadn't been fishing since—wow, was it really twenty years? More like twenty-five, actually. Anyway, he was much, much too young for her. When she had last gone fishing, he wasn't even a teenager yet. How strange it was, to be that much older than a grown man, and still feel the juices rise. She remembered something her mother said once, about looking in a mirror and wondering who that old woman was. "The heart stays young, Betsy," she'd said. And so it did.

Was Morrie surprised at the silver-haired man who looked back at him during the morning shave?

How nice it would be, to hear that faint scraping sound of a man shaving again, and smell the sweet-sharp scent of aftershave newly applied! Funny the things one missed when there wasn't a man in the house.

Rats, she'd dropped a stitch. She'd only gone two stitches past it, so she unknitted two and picked it up.

She thought about her dream, about the resistant wallet. Where had that come from? Of course, from telling Morrie the story of the practical joke her mother had played when a child. People must have been awfully dumb not to have seen that string. Just as she was, in her dream, not seeing the big rubber band that yanked the wallet out of her feeble fingers.

She was getting sleepy again. She folded the needles beside each other and stuck them into the ball of yarn. Yawning, she stood and stretched a kink out of her shoulders.

"A-row?" asked Sophie.

"Back to bed, Sophie," said Betsy. "Let's hope I don't go running after any more wallets in my dreams."

She massaged her scalp vigorously as she started back to her bedroom. Then she stopped.

Could it be?

"Ra-arow?" asked Sophie.

Betsy needed to talk to someone who spoke English. But who, at four forty-five?

"Jill!" Betsy said. Jill was still on nights at present, a thankless job in a sedate and orderly town like Excelsior; perhaps she might welcome an interruption. Jill carried a personal cell phone, which she could turn off while giving someone a ticket or taking part in an arrest. Betsy dialed the number and was pleased when she got a gruff, "Yeah?"

"Jill, it's me, Betsy. Have you got a minute?"

"What on earth are you doing up at this hour?"

"I think I know what happened to Paul. It all depends on where the gun is."

"What gun?"

"The gun Paul used to shoot Angela, and which was used on him."

"I thought no one knew where it is."

"I think I do. But you'll need to get a search warrant."

"I can't ask for a search warrant; I'm not an investigator. Anyway I'm not assigned to the case."

"Who is?"

"Mike for Angela's murder, someone in Orono for Paul's. What happened, what did you find out?"

"I went out to dinner with Morrie last night and then I had this dream about a wallet."

"Betsy, why don't you go back to bed and get some more sleep?" Jill could remember another time when Betsy got all excited about a conclusion she'd reached based mostly on wishful thinking and exhaustion.

"No, it's almost time for me to get up anyway, I have water aerobics this morning."

"Then tell me what it is you think you've figured out."

And Betsy did.

Jill, a patient listener, didn't interrupt. When Betsy was done, Jill said, "What if the gun isn't there?"

"Well, then, it's all snow on my boots. Gone with the first breath of hot air." For some reason that tickled Betsy a bit and she giggled.

"I don't know if we can get a search warrant based on just that theory."

"Then let's just go out there and ask if we can look."

"Not at this hour. No one with any brains is going to allow people to tramp all over their living room at five o'clock in the morning. Let me talk to Mike in the morning, and if he's not game, I'll call Orono PD." Orono supplied law enforcement for its three suburbs, including Navarre.

Jill must have used all her powers of persuasion—more even than Betsy used in persuading herself to follow her morning routine and drive to Golden Valley for her exercise—because when Betsy came home, there was a phone message for her from Jill. And when she and Jill drove up to Paul Schmitt's old house about nine, there were three official-looking dark cars and a squad car waiting.

Mike Malloy was beside one dark car, looking uncomfortable and grumpy. He cast a skittish eye on Betsy, then went over to say something to the blue-jowled man in an open overcoat standing nearby. The blue-jowled man looked as if he'd been sent by central casting to play the role of a police detective. As Malloy looked at Betsy and laughed, the blue-jowled man rolled his eyes and lifted his arms a little in a tired shrug. Betsy felt a twinge of doubt and wished she was as sure she was right as she'd been a few hours ago. This immediately turned into a stab of anger. Of course she was right!

Jill, still in uniform, walked over to the pair, motioning Betsy to follow. She introduced Betsy to Sergeant Fulk Graham, Orono PD, in a respectful voice, but merely nodded at Malloy.

Then Betsy saw the real reason for this turnout: Morrie Steffans, looking nonchalant until he sneaked a wink at her. A senior investigator, he had the pull to convince these people to come around. Jill must have called him. Jill went next to talk to him, and her smile had a subtle element of triumph to it when she glanced toward Betsy.

Please, please, let me be right, thought Betsy. For the first time she realized that being wrong would not only reflect badly on her, it could put a major kink in Jill's career. But she took a steadying breath and went up to Jill.

"Has anyone knocked yet?" she asked.

"No, we were waiting for you," said Mike brusquely.

"Let's get this show on the road, can we?" said the Orono detective.

Betsy went up on the porch and rang the doorbell. She had phoned the house early this morning and caught Mrs. Searles in the confusion of trying to get her children out in time to catch their bus, and her husband off to work. Yes, she would be at home today, and yes, Betsy could come out and if Kaitlyn didn't stop feeding her toast to Toby, there would be no toast for her in this house ever again.

The kids had departed, as had the husband. The house was warm and smelled of bread rising and Lemon Pledge. Mrs. Searles had left the fireplace alone, as instructed. Morrie had a flashlight, but so did Betsy, and Mike, and Jill, and the Orono cop.

It was Morrie, being slim and having long arms, who got to twist himself between the glass doors and shine a flashlight up the chimney. He grunted and came back out, soot marring the snowy white of his shirt sleeves.

"There's something up there, all right," he said. "Looks like a cord of some sort. But no gun."

Mike frowned, but didn't say anything. He'd been

228

wrong about the gates and just the presence of the cord was a point in Betsy's favor.

"Isn't there a ledge up there?" asked Jill. "You know, where the chimney narrows."

Morrie put the flashlight down on the hearth and twisted himself back into the firebox, one long arm reaching upward. There was a scrabbling, scraping sound as he fumbled for the ledge—and a surprised grunt when he found something.

He came back out with a large and very dirty semi-automatic pistol in a filthy hand. "Heck of a hiding place," he noted. "Might've gone off and hurt someone."

"Son of a bitch!" said Malloy.

"The one place we didn't think to look," said Fulk, staring hard at Malloy.

The slide was very resistant, but at last yielded and showed the gun to be empty.

"He used the last bullet on himself, because he didn't want it to go off and show people where it went," said Betsy.

"Who didn't?" asked Mrs. Searles, staring at the weapon.

"Paul Schmitt," said Betsy.

17

"I will work here forever," promised Godwin, right hand raised, "but only if you tell us *everything*." He was sitting at the library table, his lunch of a chef's salad—dressing on the side—forgotten in the excitement. Beside him was Shelly, a schoolteacher who worked part time during the school year—she was supposed to be at a teacher's conference today but called in sick when Betsy phoned to ask her to work.

Shelly had planned to miss just the morning sessions, but when Betsy came in all cock-a-hoop with news of a resolution, she decided the heck with it.

Jill was also present, tired but smiling, as were Alice and Martha. Betsy had called Alice on her way back from Navarre, asking her to come in for a "vindication." Alice had phoned Martha, who drove them both over.

And Foster Johns, sitting very still in a chair at the other end of the table from Betsy—but his stillness was that of a bottle of beer shaken hard and its open top covered with a thumb.

"It was Paul who murdered Angela," began Betsy. "He went through the basement from the gift shop to the bookstore."

"Wait a minute, wait a minute," said Martha. "I don't understand about Paul going through the basement. If it was that simple, how did Mike miss it?"

"The gift shop, the pet store, and the bookstore are all in one building," said Betsy.

"Yes, I know, it's the Tonka Building," said Martha. "That corner store started life as a Ford dealership, back in the late forties, early fifties."

"Anyway," said Betsy, "there's one basement under all three stores. Then some owner decided each store should have its own storage area, and put up board walls. But they cut gates through them, probably in case of fire, or so that if someone later joined two stores together, he could use all the space without having to come upstairs to get from one part to the next. But after that, someone nailed the gates shut, possibly to prevent theft."

"But if the gates were nailed shut, how did Paul get from the gift shop to the bookstore?" asked Shelly.

"Paul pulled the nails," said Betsy.

"And no one noticed?" asked Martha.

"No, because on his way back to his shop after he shot Angela, he put screws in the same holes, using rusty screws from his collection in his home woodworking shop so they'd look like they'd been in place for years. I noticed there were screws holding the gates shut even though everyone kept saying the gates were nailed shut. That didn't prove he killed her, but it broke his alibi."

"That's better than Mike could do," said Godwin.

"That's right," said Alice.

Betsy continued, "And when Mike Malloy searched the bookstore for clues, he missed another one, the shell casing that flew out of the pistol when Paul fired it. Paul needed that casing found to complete his frame-up of Foster Johns."

"Why?" asked Martha.

"Because when he shot Angela, the bullet went out the window and disappeared. The police can compare slugs, and Paul wanted it understood that the same gun that killed Angela was used in another murder. But shell casings are almost as good, and Mike didn't find the casing that flew out of Paul's gun when he shot Angela."

"But they did find a casing," objected Shelly. "In fact, they found two of them."

"No, at first Mike couldn't find any. Then after Paul was shot, and shell casings were found, he went back and looked again. This time he found one. The second one was found when the bookstore replaced some shelving. But only one bullet was fired in the shop."

"I don't understand," said Alice.

"Remember when Comfort said she saw Paul's ghost? That wasn't a ghost, that was Paul, planting a shell casing. Mike hadn't found the first one and Paul needed it found so he could frame Foster for the murder."

"Foster was *framed?*" exclaimed Martha. "You mean, he didn't murder Paul, either?"

"No, he didn't."

"*Hah!*" exclaimed Alice, smacking the surface of the table with a large hand.

"It was just what everyone thought it was when they heard Paul was dead," said Betsy. "A murder-suicide. Paul shot Angela and then himself. But he decided to play one last vicious practical joke by framing someone else for both deaths."

"Oh, are you *sure?*" asked Martha in a terrible voice.

"Yes," said both Betsy and Jill together.

"Oh, but . . . Oh, that's terrible, because . . ." She bit her underlip and fell silent.

Betsy continued, "I think Paul first intended the police to think Angela was killed in a robbery, but when he shot her, the bullet went out through the front window, drawing immediate attention, so he fled down the stairs, pausing only long enough to drive a wood screw into the nail hole on the pet store side, so when Mike went down there, the gate was fastened shut. If Paul had taken time to break the lock on the back door, the notion of a robbery gone wrong might still have been a logical theory. But the back door *is* all the way at the back, and the stairs to the basement are behind the checkout counter, right where he was standing, and people were running toward the store.

"So Mike was left assuming Angela let someone in, which meant she was shot by someone she knew. The logical suspect was the husband, Paul. But Paul had a bone-dry alibi—which would hold only until Mike figured out the business with the screws. Paul was sure Mike would figure it out and come to arrest him. And he *deserved* to be arrested, he'd murdered the one woman he'd loved in all his life. His solution to his dilemma was to take his own life and frame someone he hated for both deaths."

"But the murder weapon disappeared—" began Martha.

"It's been found," said Jill. "But let her tell the story in her own way."

Betsy said, "Now to Paul, the real cause of Angela's murder was her adultery with the man who'd made a fool of him, the man who had stolen the love of his life: Foster Johns.

"Another obsessed man might have simply gone over and shot Foster before going home to shoot himself. But Paul was different. Once before, he'd caught a man kissing his wife. Just a consoling kiss, on the occasion of his mother-in-law's funeral. But Paul couldn't handle even that slight threat to his possessive pride. And while this perhaps wasn't a killing offense, the man needed to be taught a lesson."

"God knows what he did to Angela for it," remarked Foster, speaking for the first time.

"Yes," said Betsy, and there was a small, dark pause. Then she continued, "Paul began telling the man lies about his father's offer to bring the man and his brother into his business. He told the father lies, he told the brothers lies, egging each on. When the quarrels started, he suggested to the father and brother what to say in explanation, and then told the man what lies of explanation would be told. When the man was totally estranged from his brother and father, he began to play the same game with the man and his wife. Paul was murdered before the man and his wife divorced, and things started coming around right for him. The man talked to his wife and began to understand what a filthy trick had been played on him—and by whom. He told me he would never cease being grateful to the person

234

who murdered Paul. The man, who was by nature a loyal person, watched his whole life wrench apart in a series of betrayals, and had actually begun to feel he was going insane."

"Who was the man?" asked Martha.

"It's not important, he had nothing to do with Paul's death."

"Does he live here in Excelsior?" asked Shelly.

"Not anymore."

Alice sighed and looked away. "Is there no end to the pain he caused?" she murmured.

Martha said, "Is there anything we can do to help?"

"I don't think so," said Betsy.

Shelly said, "Go on, Betsy, tell us the rest."

"There are four things about Paul that helped me figure this out. First, he had an unusual capacity for pain. Gretchen Tallman stomped hard on his instep when he put unwelcome hands on her, and it didn't deter him, the way it would any normally-wired man. And back when he was in middle school, he broke his arm and detoured from the nurse's office to frighten his teacher by waving the injury under her nose."

"Why would he do that?" asked Shelly.

"For the pleasure of seeing her shocked face. He knew the arm looked horrible, but it didn't hurt enough to make him hurry to get it taken care of."

"Ick," said Shelly.

"Second," continued Betsy, "he was very fond of true crime stories. Third, he loved cruel practical jokes. And fourth, he was clever at laying the blame for his misdoings at the feet of others."

Jill said, "The first explains how he came to be so beat up, right? Most people couldn't endure hurting themselves enough to cause bruises, at least after the first one."

"But he was shot more than once," Martha pointed out. "I understand being shot is extraordinarily painful."

"He was very angry," said Betsy, "very determined."

"Okay, what's the true crime angle?" asked Alice.

Betsy said, with an air of confession, "I read a lot of true crime stories myself when I was in high school, and I don't think I've ever lost my taste for them."

"So I guess I'm not the only person here who loves the forensics shows on the Learning Channel," said Martha.

"Hush," said Godwin. "She's getting to the good part now, I bet."

Betsy continued, "Last night I went out to dinner with Morrie and somehow we got to talking about a very old-fashioned prank involving a wallet and a length of button thread. And when I went to bed, I kept dreaming of a wallet that jumped out of my hands whenever I tried to pick it up. And that finally reminded me of one of those old true crime stories. There was a man who was determined to commit suicide, but he'd recently taken out a large life insurance policy that had a suicide clause. So he bought a long and thick elastic band and fastened one end up a chimney and the other end to his gun. After he shot himself, the gun was pulled from his hand up the chimney. It wasn't until the house was torn down years later that the gun was found, and the truth discovered."

Godwin said, "Is that what Paul did?"

Betsy nodded. "He used a bungee cord. The gun broke a chunk of brick off the hearth as it rushed by on its way up the chimney. The fireplace had been converted to gas, but there was still enough heat to eventually rot the cord. But the gun fell onto a ledge. Morrie found it there a few hours ago. The police are satisfied with my explanation, and will mark Angela's and Paul's deaths as a murder-suicide and close the case."

Foster said, very quietly, "Thank you, Ms. Devonshire." The thumb had come off to find the beer cool and calm.

Betsy said, "When Morrie crawled up inside that chimney, we all held our breath. He was there long enough that I thought he couldn't find anything. He came out covered in soot with a piece of crumbly bungee cord and a rusty old gun."

Jill said, "It was a .45 semi-automatic. The serial number on it matches the number on the gun registration made by Paul Schmitt."

Godwin jumped to his feet and spread his arms wide. "I have said it before, and I say it again, you are the very *cleverest* person I know! I wish we had a rare wine in the place, but we don't. May I bring you a cup of tea instead, my lady?" He executed an elaborate bow.

"Yes, please," said Betsy, suddenly aware her throat was parched.

Alice said, "We will have to do something extremely

nice for you, Mr. Johns. We have to make sure everyone knows you are innocent of the murders of Angela and Paul Schmitt."

"How about we start right now," said Martha. "Alice, Shelly, let's go have a cup of coffee and a sandwich at the Waterfront Café. My treat. We can talk over what we just heard, nice and loud."

Jill yawned hugely and said she had to go home to bed.

Foster said he had work to do. He wrung Betsy's hand for a time longer than courtesy demanded, then left without another word.

Betsy, smiling, watched him go. Excelsior was a gossipy town, and Gossip Central was the Waterfront Café. Before the sun went down, the word would have spread all over town. Foster Johns's long nightmare was over.

Center Point Publishing
600 Brooks Road • PO Box 1
Thorndike ME 04986-0001 USA

(207) 568-3717

US & Canada:
1 800 929-9108